WHEN YOU GET THE CHANCE

Tom Ryan and Robin Stevenson

RP | TEENS
PHILADELPHIA

For Graeme, the best kind of friend.—TR

To C, with so much love.
You are the best, and I am the luckiest.—RS

Running Press Teens
Hachette Book Group
1290 Avenue of the Americas, New York, NY 10104
www.runningpress.com/rpkids
@RP_Kids

Printed in the United States of America

First Edition: May 2020

Published by Running Press Teens, an imprint of Perseus Books, LLC, a subsidiary of Hachette Book Group, Inc. The Running Press Teens name and logo is a trademark of the Hachette Book Group.

The Hachette Speakers Bureau provides a wide range of authors for speaking events. To find out more, go to www.hachettespeakersbureau.com or call (866) 376-6591.

The publisher is not responsible for websites (or their content) that are not owned by the publisher.

Print book cover and interior design by Frances J. Soo Ping Chow.

Library of Congress Control Number: 2019936927

ISBNs: 978-0-7624-9500-9 (hardcover), 978-0-7624-9501-6 (ebook)

LSC-C

10 9 8 7 6 5 4 3 2 1

CHAPTER ONE
MARK

I love flying.

It's glamorous, almost make-believe, even. You take a seat and then float through the clouds, arriving in a few short hours at a destination that would take days to travel by car, weeks by bike, months or even years by foot.

"Look," I say, leaning past my sister Paige to point out the window. "There's Toronto."

Halifax is already a distant memory, although we've only been in the air for a couple of hours. I'm not sure when I started to get annoyed at how small Halifax is, but my feelings were confirmed when we took off this morning, the entire peninsula visible through the window before we were even at half altitude. I don't care if it *is* the biggest city on the East Coast. If you can walk around the entire thing in an afternoon, that counts as tiny by my standards.

Toronto, on the other hand . . .

"See," I say, moving my finger from landmark to landmark, "that's the CN Tower, where Drake is sitting on the cover of that album. The building next to it that looks like a giant boob is Rogers Centre, where Beyoncé plays when she comes to town." I say all this as if they're places I visit on a regular basis, when the truth is I haven't been to Toronto since I was ten.

"It's big," she says.

"No kidding. It's easily Canada's biggest city. Over two and a half million people. Everything is bigger in Toronto. Every kind of restaurant you can imagine, unbelievable shopping, the biggest film festival in North America."

"You should write for the city tourism board," she says.

"Maybe I will," I say. "I'm totally moving here after high school. It'll be epic. In the meantime, I'll settle for being in town for Pride. It's the—"

"Let me guess," she says. "It's the biggest Pride festival in Canada."

"You're pretty sarcastic for a ten-year-old," I say.

"I can't help the way I am," she says. "So you're going to try to make it to Pride? Have you run this past Mom yet?"

We both glance briefly at our mother, who is sitting in the aisle seat. Her earbuds are in, and she's engrossed in some boring dramatic movie about serious people during some serious war. On the tiny screen, Kate Winslet, in the frumpiest overcoat ever, is running alongside a train in a snowy landscape, tears streaming down her face. *Save your breath,* I think, *there's bound to be another one in a few hours.*

"I haven't mentioned it yet," I say, "but she has no problem with me going to Pride in Halifax, so why should she have a problem with me going here? Especially since we're lucky enough to be on this trip in the first place."

"Lucky?" asks Paige. "Do you even remember why we're here?"

"Of course I do," I say, although I can feel myself blushing. "Obviously, that's not what I mean by lucky. Don't get me wrong, it's super sad, it's just that until last week we didn't know we were going to be in Toronto, and now here we are. Funeral is priority number one, obvs, but after that we're sticking around, so I don't see why we shouldn't take advantage of it."

A couple of days ago, we got a call from a neighbor of our grandparents, informing us that our grandfather—Mom's father— had died. This was a shock because Grandpa was in great health. When he and Grandma visited us at Christmas, he was as fun and energetic as he was when I was a little kid. Grandma, on the other hand, was in really rough shape physically, and she found the traveling difficult. After they left, Mom and Dad had a lot of serious conversations about Grandma and what was going to happen next. Nobody expected that something would happen to Grandpa first.

Anyway, it's very sad, and Mom's been a bit of a mess. Plans came together quickly, though: a flight to Toronto for Grandpa's

3

funeral, and then we are going to spend a couple of weeks with my grandmother at the condo.

Even though Dad couldn't get the time off work, Mom has been passing it off as a "family vacation by necessity"—making the best out of a sad situation. She's been saying for years that we should come up and spend some time with my grandparents before one of them is gone. Too late, I guess, and although she has been trying to act positive about the trip, I know she feels kind of guilty.

"What's their house like, anyway?" Paige asks.

"They don't live in a house," I tell her. "They moved to a condo a few years ago. I was in their old house a couple of times, the one Mom grew up in, but I don't really remember it. We were usually at the cottage when we came to Ontario."

"Are we going there?" she asks. "To the cottage?"

"No," I tell her. "There's too much going on in the city. Mom is going to be helping Grandma with paperwork and stuff like that. We'll do lots of cool stuff in the city, you'll see. The cottage is kind of boring anyway. You're too young to remember."

I don't know what made me say that. I don't remember it that way at all, to be honest. We travelled to the cottage in Muskoka for two weeks every summer from the time I was a baby until I was ten, and none of those memories are boring.

I'm not sure why we stopped going to the cottage. I started playing soccer seriously, which meant summers got really busy and scheduled. Mom started her own practice, and Dad began working at home to help take care of us. I guess I never really thought about it. One summer came and went without the annual trip to Ontario, and then that was just the way things were.

I remember Grandpa taking us out in the canoe to the far corners of the lake, where we might glide silently past herons or a family of deer. Once we saw a bear and its cubs eating berries from a bush. If I took a ride like that today, my phone would be in constant action, shot after shot, Instagram lighting up with new hearts faster than I could post photos. Back then, though, it was good enough to just look at the animals, and I find that I'm able to conjure the images up in my mind as clearly as if it were last summer.

Of course, I was really sad to hear that Grandpa had died, but now, thinking about how much he used to love spending time with us at the lake, I get a hard lump in my throat.

"Forget I said that," I tell Paige, a sudden burst of regret that I've mischaracterized the cottage. "It wasn't boring. It was great. We spent a lot of time in the water, and at night we would have campfires and make s'mores. Sometimes Talia and I would walk along the dirt road to the canteen to get ice cream."

"Who's Talia?" she asks.

"Our cousin," I say, surprised. "Don't you remember her?"

She shakes her head.

"She's Uncle Gary's daughter. They were always at the cottage when we visited, but I guess we haven't seen her in years."

Her face screws up, trying to remember. "Uncle Gary is Mom's brother, right?"

I stare at her, trying to figure out if she's joking, but it's a genuine question.

"Yeah," I tell her. "He's her older brother. Her only sibling, like me and you."

How can she not know for sure about Uncle Gary or Talia? I know she was only a toddler when we were last at the cottage, but still, they're Mom's closest family, after Grandma and Grandpa. Even as I'm recognizing how weird this is, I start to wonder when Mom last mentioned anything about Gary or Talia, and I draw a blank. I mentally scan the family pictures on the wall in the den: Grandma and Grandpa; Dad's parents, Nanna and Pops; his brothers and their families; and of course loads of me and Paige at all ages. But none of Uncle Gary and Talia. How have I never noticed this?

"Mom," I say, poking her in the arm.

She presses the screen on the back of the seat in front of her, pausing her movie, and pulls out her earbuds. "What's up, Marky Mark?"

I hate that nickname. I don't think she realizes how much it dates her. "Are Uncle Gary and Talia going to be at the funeral?"

A strange look flickers across her face and is gone as quickly as it appears.

"Yes," she says. "Your grandmother tells me that they'll be staying at a hotel close to the condo."

"Haven't you spoken to Uncle Gary since Grandpa died?"

She smiles at me, but something about her expression is false. "No. I haven't had the chance. Things have been so busy. We'll see them at the memorial service this afternoon."

The pilot comes on the intercom.

"Hi, there, folks. We'll be starting our descent to Pearson International in just a few minutes. Weather in Toronto is sunny and clear, with an average temperature of twenty-five degrees."

It could be cool, I think to myself, to see Talia again. I wonder what she's been up to since we were kids. I make a mental note to look her up online. I wonder if she likes to party. Maybe she'll want to come out and hang at Pride with me. Talia is a year ahead of me in school, so she'll have just graduated. If both of us go, maybe Mom will see it as safer somehow. Maybe Talia will count as a chaperone, not that I need one.

I smile to myself. By tomorrow, the stress and sadness of the funeral will be over, and I'll have more than a week to spend in Toronto. I checked the weather forecast before leaving, and the nice weather is supposed to last right through the weekend; perfect for Pride.

I close my eyes and imagine the excitement of Pride in an honest-to-god big city; music, dancing, good vibes, and cute boys everywhere, the perfect conditions for a summer romance. But my smile fades as my thoughts drift uncomfortably to Jareth, and I wonder for the hundredth time whether I've been clear enough with him about where we stand. I mean, we never officially started dating, so that should mean there's no need to officially call things off, right?

Jareth is a great guy: good-looking, funny, and nice. Too nice, to be honest. We've been seeing each other for a few months, ever since a friend introduced us at a party. There was a spark there, for sure, but lately I've found myself ignoring more and more of his texts and looking for excuses not to hang out. The problem is, he hasn't gotten the hint, and I've been too much of a chickenshit to tell him how I really feel.

I tell myself that out of sight is out of mind, and that a bit of distance will be good for Jareth. A couple of weeks on his own, without contact, and he's bound to get the idea and move on. With some luck, by the time I return to Halifax, I'll have a bunch of stories for my friends, and Jareth will be nothing more than a thing from the past, fuzzier in my mind than those childhood memories of bears and herons.

CHAPTER TWO
TALIA

Old age is terrifying. It's only been three years, but I barely recognize my grandmother. She's bent over and looks so frail. I swear she must've shrunk six inches since I was last in Toronto. "Talia," she says, gazing up at me. "You look so like Gary. That lovely thick hair."

I smile because she's being kind and because it's her husband's funeral, so she can say whatever she likes. But really? My father is almost bald.

She turns away to greet someone else, and my father and I slide into one of the narrow wooden pews.

We're at Greenhaven Funeral Home, but there's nothing green about it: It's a small, windowless, airless room, and it couldn't be more generic or more depressing. When I die, I want people to gather in the woods or at a beach or something. Scatter my ashes, share a bottle of wine, tell some stories.

Dad nudges me. "You okay?"

I nod. "I guess. You?"

"Still can't quite believe it," he says. "But yes, I'm fine. Worried about my mother, mostly."

"She looks really old," I whisper, twisting in my seat to look back at her. "Hey, who's that talking to her? Is that Mark and Paige? And my . . . Aunt . . . Janet?" I wonder if she'll expect me to call her Aunt Janet. It sounds too weird. And it's not like she's going to call me Niece Talia. It's one of those weird hierarchical things that I try to avoid.

He glances over. "Yes." He doesn't get up to greet them or anything, which seems kind of rude. I don't even know when he last saw his sister. I think they had a fight years ago, or some kind of falling out or something. Anyway, they don't ever talk.

Last time I saw my cousins, we were all just kids. I haven't been to my grandparents' cottage since the summer before grade seven. I remember that summer so vividly—swimming in the cold lake, eating ice cream, pretending that the abandoned cottage down the road was haunted, trying to catch a fish and freaking out when we succeeded and didn't know how to get the hook out of the poor creature's mouth. It died, and I cried my eyes out. Mark thought we should cook it for dinner but I talked him into a fish funeral. There's probably still a cross in the woods: *R.I.P. FISH.*

I think that summer at the cottage stands out in my memory because those were my last weeks of really being a kid. Grade seven was when everything got complicated: I got my period the first week of school, and it was all downhill from there.

My memory of Mark is of a wiry, sun-tanned boy in shorts and not much else—all ribs and knees and elbows. Now he's six feet tall and good-looking. Actually, he's not just good-looking: more like could-be-a-model gorgeous.

To be honest, I have a bit of an automatic negative reaction to people who are that good-looking. I know this is totally not fair, and, in general, I think it's a really bad idea to assume anything based on something as superficial as looks . . . but in my experience, people who are really good-looking often know it and are actually jerks. Or at best, they are used to everyone treating them a certain way and they just think the world is like that for everyone. But it's not.

As I'm watching, Paige leans against Mark and he puts an arm around her and gives her a really sweet smile, and she grins up at him. I can't help smiling, too. She's super cute, and seeing Mark being all affectionate to her makes me feel more warmly toward him. Also more curious. I wonder what he's like now. I pull out my phone and start searching MARK DAWSON HALIFAX.

Dad elbows me. *"Talia.* Put that away."

I sigh and slip my phone back into my jacket pocket. "What's going to happen with the cottage? Will Grandma keep it?"

He shakes his head. "That's something I need to talk to her about. I hate to bring it up, but I can't see her managing it on her own. All the upkeep. How would she even get there? She doesn't drive anymore. And I can't help her as much as I'd like to. Victoria is just too far away."

Tell me about it. Erin said exactly that just two weeks ago, during what I guess you'd call our big breakup. We were supposed to have the whole summer together—our post-high-school grad summer, our last summer before university—and we had a million plans. We were even planning this fund-raising event for our school's GSA—Gender and Sexuality Alliance. Erin and I were the cofounders and had been leading the group for three years, so this was supposed to be a kind of parting gift for the younger students who'd be taking over from us. Then Erin got offered a job in Toronto, in their older brother's coffee shop right at Church and Wellesley, which is the beating rainbow heart of Toronto's gay village, and decided to dump me and all our plans.

"I'm not saying we should break up," Erin whispered. We'd been in my bed all afternoon, alternately fighting and cuddling and making out, which is just all kinds of messed up. *"I just think that Victoria and Toronto are so far apart, and we should both be free to do what we want. Long-distance relationships are hard. And we've talked about having a more open relationship, right? So maybe this is a good time to try that. See how it goes."*

"Yeah. While I'm stuck here in Victoria with the same people we've known forever, and you're working in a queer cafe

in *Canada's queer epicenter."* I pulled away from them. *"That sounds like a great time to try it."*

"Don't be like that."

"Like what? You're the one who's leaving."

"Leaving Victoria. Not leaving you."

"Well, since I'm staying in Victoria, it's kind of the same thing, isn't it?"

Erin looked at me. *"I was going anyway in the fall, for school."*

"Which is why spending this summer together was so important!" Erin had gotten into the University of Toronto. Dad said we couldn't afford for me to live away from home, so I was going all the way to (drumroll please) the University of Victoria, a twenty-minute bike ride from the house I'd lived in for my entire life. *"At least it was to me. Apparently not so much to you."*

Erin was blinking away tears and their face was flushed. *"Do you want to break up? Is that what you're saying?"*

"It's not what I'm saying. It's what you're doing."

"Talia?" Dad puts his hand on my knee and squeezes it. "Are you okay?"

I brush away a tear. "Fine."

"I know it's sad. Just keep in mind, he had a really good life. And I know this was a shock, but I think he would've chosen to go quickly. He always said that—that he hoped when the time came, it'd be—"

"It's not that," I say. "I mean, yeah, it is sad, but—"

"Is it what I said about the cottage?" He frowns. "I didn't realize it was that important to you. I guess you have a lot of memories from those summers."

"Not really. I mean, yes, I remember it, but I don't care if it gets sold or whatever." I feel a bit shallow, given where we are, but I never lie to my dad. Almost never, anyway. "I was just thinking about Erin."

"Oh." His face softens. Dad loves Erin; we were together for almost three years. I haven't actually told him we have sort of maybe broken up, but he may have guessed. "Will you see her? While we're here?"

"Them," I remind him. "Will I see *them*. And, no, probably not."

"Sorry. Them," he says. He hesitates, like he wants to ask what's going on with us but doesn't want to pry. "Well, if you change your mind . . . We have two weeks in Toronto."

Steady streams of people are still flowing into the room, the pews filling up. Mark and Paige and Janet slide into a pew on the opposite side of the room, and I see Janet glance our way and then quickly avert her gaze. She's wearing a short skirt and boots, and she has the same unruly red-brown hair as I do. Mark and Paige both have straight dark hair and look nothing like their mom.

Dad looks over at his sister and his forehead wrinkles deepen. "Actually," he says, "maybe we won't spend the whole

14

time in Toronto. I wonder if you and I should go up to the cottage. I bet it needs a lot of cleaning up before it can be sold, and I can't see my mother being able to manage that on her own."

We just got into Toronto late last night. Checked into our hotel, got room service, and watched a movie. Slept in. Had a late lunch. Came here. We haven't even been to my grandmother's condo yet and he's already planning to leave? And I know I just told him that I wasn't planning to see Erin, but I was still kind of hoping that I might. I sent a text this morning: Surprise. In Toronto for two weeks. I check my phone again: still no reply.

"What's the plan for this evening?" I ask. "Are we having dinner with Grandma?"

He nods. "She wants us all there. Janet, me, you kids."

I sneak another glance at my cousins and catch Mark looking right at me. He gives a wave and a grin, and I wave back, feeling awkward. "Dad?" I whisper. "What's up with you and Janet, anyway?"

"What do you mean?"

"You know. How come you never talk to her? Or, like, talk about her?"

He tugs on his tie—he never wears ties, normally—and it makes him look like he's wearing a costume. "We're not close."

"Duh, obviously. Did something happen? You had a fight?"

"Siblings don't always get along, you know." He doesn't look at me. "Only children always seem to imagine that having a

15

brother or sister would be this wonderful thing, but there's no guarantee that you'll see eye to eye, Talia."

"Uh, this isn't about me being an only child, Dad. I just wondered why you and Janet don't get along."

"I don't really want to get into it."

"Get into *what*?" Now I am curious. "Like, do you just not like her? Or . . ." But I can remember them at the cottage together, my dad and Janet and my grandparents, all four of them sitting on the deck, drinking wine and playing card games. "Why did we stop going to the cottage anyway?" I don't know why I've never questioned this before. The first year we didn't go, Dad said Grandma was having hip replacement surgery, and then . . . we just never went back.

"Talia." Dad swivels to face me. "This is my father's memorial service. My *father*. And this is not something I want to discuss."

I swallow. "Sorry."

Could I be any more insensitive, seriously? Obviously, this isn't the time to ask him. Sometimes I really suck.

A middle-aged man in one of those minister's collar things walks to the front of the room, taps on the mic, clears his throat. The voices gradually die down and the room falls silent.

I steal another glance at Mark. I wonder if he knows what the deal with our parents is.

CHAPTER THREE

MARK

The memorial is just what you'd expect. Some tears, a few nice speeches, and some awkward mingling. I'm hoping to chat with Gary and Talia, but I get stuck in a conversation about the East Coast with a friendly old woman who used to teach with Grandpa. By the time I'm able to break away, they're on the other side of the room, giving Grandma hugs and then disappearing from the funeral home altogether.

Afterward, we share a cab with Grandma to her condo. The building is huge, at least twenty stories, but her condo is really small and swelteringly hot. It also smells incredible, which explains the heat.

"Mom," says my mother as we file into the small hallway behind Grandma. "Are you cooking a turkey?"

"Yes," says Grandma, bustling into the apartment ahead of us. "I put it in before I left for the service. If you'll give me a moment, I just want to check on it."

"It's the middle of the summer," Mom says with disbelief, but Grandma is already heading into the kitchen, opening and closing doors and drawers with efficiency. She's obviously happy to be back in her own space, and I'm glad to see that she seems a bit less confused than she did at the memorial service, where she barely recognized me.

Mom hurries around, opening windows, and Paige and I explore the tiny condo. Besides the kitchen and a combined living and dining room, there's one bathroom, a balcony with two chairs and a couple of potted tomatoes, and a small guest room, which Mom and Paige will be sharing.

"You're on the couch, Mark," says Mom, and I force myself not to complain. I doubt I'll be doing any sleeping in, and I might as well forget about privacy altogether.

Mom heads into the kitchen to help Grandma with dinner, and Paige flops into a chair with her book. I pull my phone out, and—surprise, surprise—there's another text from Jareth.

Hope everything's going okay with your family! So sad :(call me later if you need to talk my shift's over at 5

I close my eyes and take a yoga breath. I know he's trying to be considerate, but he's just so much work. I don't have the energy to text him back right now. Instead, I wander around the living room, checking out the many framed paintings and certificates and photographs that cover every available square inch of wall space.

I stop at one photo and smile, recognizing me and Talia at the cottage. We're standing on the dock with our arms draped around each other, beaming at the camera.

The doorbell rings.

"That'll be Gary and Talia," says Grandma, sticking her head out of the kitchen.

I notice Mom's neck and shoulders tighten. "I thought you told me they were staying at a hotel," she says. She's trying to sound nonchalant, but I know all the signs of Mom's anxiety, and they are quickly converging.

"They are," says Grandma, wiping her hands on her apron and heading toward the door, "but I invited them for supper. Obviously." Her tone is crisp and assertive, as if she knows that she has to nip something in the bud.

"Of course," says Mom. She takes a deep breath and follows Grandma into the hallway. Paige and I exchange a glance. "What the heck?" Paige mouths. I shrug, and we follow them.

Gary and Talia enter, smiling awkwardly. They hug Grandma, and then Gary turns to Mom.

"Good to see you, Janet," he says.

"Yes. You, too," she says.

They move together haltingly, then lean in for a short, uncomfortable hug while the rest of us stand around pretending everything is just totally normal and delightful, which it most definitely isn't. Gary shakes my hand as Mom hugs Talia, and Paige stands off to the side, more curious than shy.

"Come in," says Grandma, shooing us into the living room. She heads back into the kitchen, and the rest of us continue to stand around uncertainly. It must be the most uncomfortable family get-together on record.

"We brought wine," says Gary. He pulls a bottle from his backpack and places it on the table. Mom beelines for it gratefully. She loves to talk about wine.

"Okanagan," she says, examining the bottle. "So many great wines coming out of that region these days."

"Yes," says Gary, warming slightly. "This pinot is one of our favorites. I have to say, I was at a tasting of Nova Scotia whites a few months ago, and I was really impressed."

"Oh, yes," says Mom. "There are some wonderful little wineries in the Annapolis Valley."

I've heard that alcohol is a social lubricant, but I always assumed you had to drink it first. Still, I'm just happy that they're having a conversation, even if there is something very strange about seeing siblings behave like strangers. Paige takes advantage of the opportunity to escape and drops back into her chair with her book.

Talia is skirting the room, looking at pictures, and I join her. I point at the one of the two of us.

"You remember?" I ask.

She stares at the picture and laughs. "Wow," she says. "Look at us! Hard to believe it was only a few years ago. We were such kids."

I take her in. She's pretty tall, with a sturdy build. She has thick, red-brown hair, held back under a bandana, and about a million freckles. She's wearing cargo shorts and a tie-dyed T-shirt from some music festival. Head-to-toe granola, typical West Coast. There's something else, too, just kind of a feeling I get.

"So," I ask her, "I'm just guessing here, but are you gay?"

She looks taken aback. "That's . . . uh, not really any of your business."

I throw my hands up, surrendering. "Hey, sorry, didn't mean to offend you. Just got a vibe, that's all. I'm gay too, or *not* too, you know what I mean."

Her face softens. "Sorry," she says. "I shouldn't be so defensive. Yeah, I'm queer."

"Cool," I say. "Maybe we should come up with some kind of special handshake or something."

She gives me a sideways smile, as if trying to figure me out, but when she speaks it is to change the subject. "Grandma looks really . . . well, kind of frail, don't you think?"

"I saw her a few months ago. Christmas." I shrug. "She looks the same."

"Last time I saw her and Grandpa, I was fifteen," Talia says. "Dad's come out to Toronto every year, but I've been busy with school and stuff, so . . ." She trails off, biting her lip. "I feel kind of bad now."

"Can we get a bit of help in here?" Grandma asks from the kitchen door.

Talia follows her into the kitchen, where my mother is carving the turkey, and begins to fill serving dishes. Gary is setting the table, and I move to help him.

"So, I hear you're a bit of a soccer star," he says, as we lay out cutlery.

"Star might be a bit of a stretch. I'm pretty good, I guess."

"I used to play," he says. "The beautiful game. Best shape I was ever in."

"That's half the reason I do it," I tell him. "Killer workout. Not to mention it's a great way to meet hot guys." He laughs.

Dinner is delicious, and Grandma is obviously happy to have family around her. After an awkward start to the evening, things have warmed up significantly, and the conversation becomes a bit more natural. Mom and Gary begin telling stories about Grandpa, and soon we're all laughing, and they finally start to look each other in the eye.

I should have known it was too good to be true.

"Mom," says Gary, as Grandma cuts into a homemade apple pie, "I know there's a lot of stuff to take care of over the next couple of weeks, but I've been wondering if you've thought about the cottage at all."

We all turn to Grandma. "Well," she says, and her voice is sad and quiet, "your father and I are supposed to be there now. We planned to spend a couple of weeks on the lake this summer, but I can't imagine going there on my own."

Mom reaches over and puts her hand on Grandma's, giving it a squeeze.

"Speaking of the cottage," she says, "I was thinking it might be nice if Mark and Paige and I went up there for a few nights, maybe on the weekend."

I stare at her, shocked. This is the first I've heard of this. The cottage? On Pride weekend?

Grandma turns to her, smiling. "Of course," she says. "It would be so nice to know it was being used this summer after all. Your father and I haven't missed a summer in almost forty years." She looks back and forth between Mom and Gary, and her expression is difficult to read. "Neither of you missed it either, until a few years ago."

"Seven," says Gary, without skipping a beat. He turns to Mom, frowning. "It's all well and good for you to drive up there and take advantage of it for a holiday, but there are more serious considerations."

"Excuse me?" asks Mom. I turn to Paige, and her eyes are wide. We both know what that phrase means.

"Mom obviously can't take care of the cottage by herself," says Gary. "We should be thinking about what to do with it.

How best to clean it out. If we get organized, we could have it on the market by the end of the month. Summer is obviously the best time to try to sell at a good price."

"I can't believe I'm hearing this," says Mom. "It's like you've already made up your mind about this, without even bringing it up first. As if it's your cottage to sell!"

"I tried to bring it up," says Gary. "Just now. I was planning on offering to head up there with Talia and get things sorted out, but you just had to jump in and make it all about yourself, as always."

I stare down at the pie in front of me, wondering if it would be inappropriate to sneak a bite.

"If you think you are going to waltz in here and start ordering us around," says Mom, her voice low and steely, "you have another think coming, Gary."

"Enough!"

We all jump as Grandma slams her hands down on the table with a lot more force than I ever would have given her credit for.

"To think that the two of you couldn't put your differences aside for one dinner," she says. "On the day that your father was buried. You should both be ashamed of yourselves."

Gary and Mom both drop their heads, as aware as the rest of us that she's absolutely right. I steal a glance at Talia across the table and realize that she's looking at me, too. She raises her eyebrow questioningly, as if I might be able to shed some light on things, but I can only shrug. I'm in the dark, too.

"This is what's going to happen," says Grandma. "We are going to eat our dessert, and then wash the dishes as if that argument didn't happen. Then Gary and Talia are going to go back to their hotel. Tomorrow morning, the five of you are going to leave for Muskoka."

Gary opens his mouth to protest, but Grandma puts her hand up. "If anyone had bothered to wait and find out what I had to contribute to this conversation, I would have told you that your father—" she looks across the table at Paige and Talia and me "—and your grandfather would have liked nothing more than to see his family spend another summer at the cottage. I wish I felt the same way, but he was always more optimistic than me. You're absolutely right, Gary. There's work to be done, and to be honest, I don't have the energy to decide what should happen with the place. So I want all of you to go there, for a week, and make that decision as a family."

She stands from the table, and it's clear that she doesn't want to hear anything else on the matter.

I know it's selfish, but I can't help wondering how I'm going to wiggle myself out of this. I'm going to be at that parade, come hell or high water.

CHAPTER FOUR

TALIA

Bracebridge is exactly halfway between the equator and the North Pole and is said to be Santa's summer home. When I was a kid, I actually believed this. We used to go to Santa's Village, which is this amusement park with all the usual rides and sno-cones, plus, you know, Santa's elves, Santa's deer, and the Santa Roller Coaster Sleigh Ride.

"Remember when we used to go here?" I ask, as we drive past the *Welcome to Bracebridge! Home of Santa's Village* sign. "With Mark and Paige and Janet?"

"Uh huh," Dad says, keeping his eyes on the road.

He's super tense, acting like he can't talk because he's driving. Never mind that we're practically the only car on the road. He's been tense since Grandma's thou-shalt-go-to-the-cottage decree last night. The funny thing was that even though both he and Janet looked horrified at the thought of a cozy family week in Muskoka, neither of them put up any argument. Like,

26

none at all. It was the first time I've really seen him and Janet as Grandma's actual *kids* instead of just as grown-ups. It was like they both got sent to their room for a time-out. I guess you don't argue with your mother on the day of your father's funeral.

Though the way Dad is acting now, you'd think we were on our way to another funeral: he's not exactly great company. I find myself wondering what the mood is like in Janet's car, which is probably on the highway somewhere behind us. Dad had insisted on leaving at the crack of dawn—to beat the traffic, he'd said. *The traffic? Or Janet?* I'd asked.

He'd shaken his head like he had no idea what I was talking about, but I was pretty sure he wanted to get to the cottage before his sister. Stake his claim. Mark his territory. Hopefully, he wouldn't actually pee on the bushes, but at this point nothing would surprise me. He seems like a stranger.

My phone vibrates in my pocket and I glance down, thinking of Erin. Always my first thought, no matter how hard I try to break the habit.

But it's not Erin: it's Mark. We didn't get much of a chance to talk last night, but we'd swapped phone numbers. Are you up yet?

Almost at the cottage actually. 20 min away. You?

Just behind you I guess. Almost at Bracebridge. Mom made us get up in the middle of the night practically. Paige says she's getting pressure sores from sitting for so long

I laugh. Yeah. Guess a three hour drive from Halifax would end up in the ocean

Hey Nova Scotia is way bigger than your little island lol

"What's so amusing?" Dad asks.

"It's Mark," I say. "They're right behind us."

Dad grunts, and I swear he actually accelerates.

"What is with you?" I challenge.

He shakes his head. "Nothing. Just . . . well, I'm not really in the mood for a week at the cottage. And there's probably fifty years' worth of accumulated stuff to sort through and get rid of before we can sell it."

"*If* we sell it," I say. "Grandma and Janet didn't sound so sure." I watch the trees flashing past, tall and green against the blue sky. My phone buzzes again.

Hey Tal. Remember the canteen? And the house we thought was haunted?

Yes! We used to scare ourselves silly, daring each other to go inside after dark. I wonder if it is still there, still empty. Probably someone's knocked it down and built something new and expensive.

And the fish funeral? His text is followed by emojis: fish on hook, crying face, praying hands.

I grin. I was just thinking about that.

If we're gonna be stuck in the woods, let's make the most of it.

Despite Dad's foul mood, despite Erin, despite everything, I feel a flicker of excitement. Like anything could happen.

———

The cottage isn't right on the water—it's on a dirt road that winds through the woods, and there's a short trail that takes you down to the lake. It's smaller than I remember, from outside: long and low, single story, with a big deck. All wood and glass. Dad unlocks the door and opens it for me to go ahead of him, and memories come flooding back.

It's kind of open concept, I guess, with a big living area with faded couches and paisley-covered chairs. A solid wood dining room table, long and narrow, and a kitchen in one corner. Kitschy artwork on the wooden walls. A hallway leads to four tiny bedrooms and one larger room—I guess Janet and Dad can fight over that, and there's a cool attic space, like a loft I guess, that you have to climb a ladder to get into.

"I remember this," I say, already scrambling up. "Mark and I used to play board games up here." And there they are, still, just like I remember: a low wooden shelf: Monopoly, Jenga, Hungry Hungry Hippos, Sorry!, Life . . . I peer through the wooden railings and watch Dad opening cupboards and closets.

"Three blenders," he says, running his hands over his mostly bald head. "So far. And decades of *National Geographic*. I can't even . . ."

The door opens and Mark bursts through. "The loft! Oh my god, I remember spending so much time up there!" He begins to climb the ladder, and Janet comes in, struggling with two large red suitcases.

"Mark," she says, putting them down with a heavy *thunk*. "Perhaps you could lend a hand?"

He meets my gaze and widens his eyes comically. "Absolutely," he says. Then in a lower voice, to me: "Jenga calls, but duty calls louder."

I follow him down the ladder. "Can I do anything, Janet?"

She smiles at me, but it's a tired and strained look. "Paige has the last bag. She's just coming."

Only she isn't. I step outside and see Paige standing beside the car and staring up at the treetops. I slip my shoes on and join her. "Pretty cool, huh? Do you remember this place at all?"

She shakes her head. "No. I hope your Dad doesn't make Grandma sell it."

"He's not going to *make* her do anything." Is this what Janet has told her? "He's just worried that she won't be able to take care of it by herself, that's all."

"But we could help her," she says earnestly.

"Maybe."

Paige shrugs, hoists the bag over her shoulder, and heads inside. I linger outside for a minute, kind of taking it all in.

It's so quiet here. Peaceful. And the air smells good—clean, fresh, and green, if that makes any sense at all. I hear a noise and turn toward it: a girl walking down the road, a white-and-brown dog bounding along at her side—dashing ahead, sniffing things, tearing back to her like it's some kind of emergency. Its ears flop up and down as it runs, and I laugh out loud.

She glances my way as she passes the end of our dirt driveway. "Hey."

"Hi." I point at the dog. "Pretty cute. Puppy?"

"Eight months, so yeah. She's still kind of nuts."

The girl is pretty cute, too: thick black hair tied back in a ponytail, big sunglasses, long brown legs in very short denim cutoffs. She's not my type at all, but she's so pretty I can't help staring. She looks how I wish I looked. She's grinning at me and her teeth are very straight and white. "You new here?" she asks. "I thought I'd met everyone around my age."

"This is my grandparents' place," I say, walking toward her. "I used to come all the time when I was a kid." I bend down and pet the dog, which immediately flops, belly-up, at my feet. "Uh, I'm Talia."

"Mariana," she says. "And the love sponge here is Rosie. So are you staying all summer, or . . ."

I shrug. "No. Not long. A week, I guess."

She frowns, two little furrows appearing between her eyebrows. Even her frown is adorable. "You don't look too happy about it."

"My grandfather just died and my grandma isn't very well, so I think we might just be cleaning up the place to sell it," I say.

"That sucks . . ." She trails off, looking over my shoulder. "Oh my. Is that your brother?"

I turn, following her gaze. Mark is standing on the deck, leaning on the railing and generally looking like he's stepped straight off the cover of some glossy country life magazine. "My cousin," I say, waving at him to join us.

He waves back and takes a step toward us, then I hear his mom yelling something and he shrugs apologetically and disappears back inside.

"Wow. Well." She hesitates, looks at me, then looks back at the door Mark just disappeared through. "Listen, there's a bunch of us getting together tonight. Me, and these two brothers whose parents own the cottage beside us, and maybe a couple of other guys." She gestures in the direction of the lake. "Down to the water, hang a right, walk for twenty, twenty-five minutes— we're almost directly across the lake. There's a fire pit . . . you can't miss us. Bring your cousin."

I wonder if I should tell her she's wasting her time going after Mark. I don't want to out him, though. I mean, I get the impression he's pretty open, but I still think people should

32

respect other people's privacy. It kind of bothered me that he came right out and asked me if I was gay. What if I wasn't comfortable answering that? Totally put me on the spot. Granted, I had wondered about him, but I wouldn't have asked. I'd have let him tell me if he wanted, when he chose to.

"What is it?" Mariana asks. "I mean, no pressure if you don't want to join us."

"No, no, I do," I say. "Sorry. I was just thinking about something."

"Great! So we'll see you later, then."

"Yeah, if we can," I say, backtracking. I'm not really into partying. I don't drink, and I suck at small talk. And the whole hanging-around-the-campfire with a group of guys drinking beer while Mariana tries to hook up with my gay cousin?

Not my idea of a good time.

CHAPTER FIVE

MARK

By the time I walk back out onto the deck, carrying some ugly stackable patio chairs, the girl with the puppy is gone.

"Who was that?" I ask Talia, as she walks back toward the deck.

"Oh, just some girl from across the lake," she says. "She was wondering if we want to go to a campfire at her place tonight."

"Awesome," I say. "Let's do it."

"I don't know," she says. "It's just her and a few guys. Probably just an excuse for them to get drunk."

"Sounds great," I say. "The grand folks have a pretty impressive liquor cabinet. I doubt anyone will notice if we sneak a couple of bottles."

She looks doubtful. "I don't drink," she says.

"That's fine," I say. "You can still come. Or would you rather stick around here and contribute to the awkward, deafening silence?"

"I guess I thought we could just hang out," she says. "Maybe play a board game or something. Help break the ice."

"Board game? You're kidding, right?" I move the chairs over to the front of the deck and unstack them so that they're facing the nicest view of the woods. "They're the adults; let them deal with their own stupid drama. Our job is to escape from family obligations and behave irresponsibly. They can play Trivial Pursuit with Paige."

"We're playing Trivial Pursuit?" asks Paige as she walks out onto the deck, her arms stretched around a stack of cushions.

"Not tonight," I say. "Talia and I are going to a party."

"I didn't say I was going," Talia says.

I don't respond. I'm not going to let her throw a wet blanket on the only chance of fun within a hundred miles.

Paige drops the cushions into their chairs and then turns to us. "You guys," she says, her voice hushed and urgent. "We have to figure out what is going on around here!"

"What do you mean?" I ask.

"I mean with Mom and Uncle Gary!" she says. "Don't you think it's weird that they're so mad at each other all the time?"

"I don't know," says Talia. "I wondered about it, but we do live on opposite ends of the country."

"Yeah," says Paige, "but you both told me that everyone used to meet here every summer. Why did that stop? There has to be a reason, right?"

"Maybe not, Paige," I say. "Sometimes people just don't get along. I remember them arguing a lot back when we were kids."

"Me too," says Talia.

"Besides," I say, "I think the main reason we stopped coming is because we just started to get busy in the summer. I had soccer, and we both had swimming lessons, and Mom and Dad were always working. It just got too complicated."

Paige's eyes narrow and she crosses her arms across her chest. "I think there's more to it, and I'm going to figure it out."

"Well, don't let us stop you, Nancy Drew," I say.

We spend the rest of the afternoon sorting out the cottage. Opening windows to clear out the mustiness, pulling sheets and pillows out of taped-up garbage bags, and giving everything a decent scrub down.

By the time supper rolls around, we're all sweaty and exhausted. I want to go for a swim, but it's dusk and the mosquitoes are so bad that we end up eating in the screened porch instead, hot dogs and a store-bought potato salad.

The conversation is channeled completely through Paige and Talia and me. Mom and Gary barely say a word to one another, not much of a surprise, as they've spent the entire day working on different parts of the cottage—quite a difficult feat, considering how small the place is. It must be exhausting to spend so much energy trying not to talk to someone who's just a few feet away at any given time.

I wonder again what happened between them, but I'm not about to ask. One thing's for sure, I'm not interested in sticking around to watch the cold war play out.

I stand up from the table and look at Talia. "You coming?" I ask.

"Where are you going?" asks Gary, surprised.

"There's a bonfire at a cottage across the lake," I say. "Talia met some girl and she invited us."

"Across the lake," repeats Mom. I'm surprised when she and Gary share a knowing glance before quickly turning their heads away. "Who is this girl?"

"I don't really know," says Talia. "Her name's Mariana."

"Are you sure you should be going to a party with strangers?" asks Gary.

"I didn't even say I was going," says Talia.

"Oh, you're going," I say. "You can't let me walk over there by myself. All those strangers; think of the terrible things that could happen if I don't have a chaperone."

Talia looks across the table at her father, who shrugs. Reluctantly, she stands.

"Don't stay out too late," Mom calls over the railing as we walk across the yard toward the lake. "Behave yourselves."

"I always behave," I call back. "Question is, how will I *choose* to behave tonight?"

Once we're out of earshot, Talia stops and turns to look at me. "Listen," she says. "I really don't appreciate the way you talked to me back there. For the record, I'll go where I want, when I want. Got it?"

"Yeah," I say, taken aback. "Got it. Sorry. I wasn't trying to be an asshole or anything."

"I didn't think you were trying to be an asshole," she says. "But guys always think they can just order women around, and I seriously don't have time for that."

"I wasn't—" I stammer, "I didn't—"

"It's fine," she says, cutting me off. "I get that you didn't even know you were doing it; that's kind of the point. But if people don't get called out for shit like that, nothing will ever change."

"Why didn't you just stay behind?" I ask.

She turns to look back at the cottage, which is disappearing into the trees. "You're probably right. It's not going to be super fun to hang out there with them. Poor Paige."

"Paige will be fine," I say. "She'll have them eating out of her hand."

Talia relaxes a bit as we walk around the lake. It's so pretty and peaceful. Other than the occasional splash from people taking an evening swim, or the chatter drifting down from people eating on their decks, the only sound is the light rustle of wind through the trees.

"So have you got, like, a girlfriend back in Victoria?" I ask her. I'm not sure, but she seems to tense up again. Maybe I shouldn't have asked.

"Not exactly," she says. "It's a bit complicated."

"You guys taking a break?" I ask.

"I guess you could say that." She doesn't volunteer anything else.

"What's her name?" I ask.

"Their name is Erin," she says, a hard emphasis on the *their*.

"Their?"

"Erin's nonbinary," she says. "Anyway, they're moving to Toronto for school this fall, but their brother has a coffee shop in the Village, so they decided to move earlier and work there for the summer."

"Must be difficult to keep them all straight," I say with a laugh. "So to speak."

"Excuse me?" she asks, stopping in her tracks. When I turn to look at her, she's got a seriously angry look on her face.

"I'm just kidding around," I say. "I never really understood the whole 'them/they' pronoun thing. Seems complicated, that's all."

"*Complicated*?" she asks. "What's *complicated* is trying to exist in a world that doesn't acknowledge your identity. What's *complicated* is dealing with people who mock the way you choose to refer to yourself. What's *complicated*—not to mention *completely exhausting*—is constantly having to push back against a world that is totally married to archaic binary ideas about gender that basically erase the existence of anyone who doesn't fit into neat little boxes."

"Jesus," I say, throwing my hands up. "I was just making a joke, I didn't think."

"That's the thing," she says. "People like you don't think because nobody expects you to."

"Hey," I say. "I'm gay, too, remember? I've dealt with my fair share of snide comments. Try playing sports when you're a gay male."

"Yeah," she says. "It must be really difficult to be an athletic, able-bodied white guy. The struggle is real."

"Whoa," I say. "Let's both calm down a bit. I'm sorry, okay? Can we be friends?"

For a minute she doesn't say anything. Then she shakes her head. "Maybe I overreacted," she says. "I've been upset about Erin leaving and I'm kind of on edge. But you need to know that kind of thing isn't cool. Life might be fun and games for you, but it's not that way for everyone."

"Totally," I say, feeling a wave of shame at how right she is, how stupid I sounded. "I was being an asshole. I should know better. I'll try harder, I promise."

"Okay," she says. "It's all right. I appreciate that."

I'm worried that she's going to turn around and head back to the cottage, but she continues walking.

"So," I say, after a couple of minutes. "Are you going to see them when you're in Toronto? Erin?"

"I don't know," she says miserably. "I guess it depends on how long we end up staying here at the lake. And whether Erin even gets in touch. I've been texting them, but haven't heard anything so far. Anyway, I don't really want to talk about it. What about you? Do you have a boyfriend?"

"Oh," I say. "Not really. I mean, I've kind of been dating this guy back home for a while, but it's super casual. Not serious at all."

I wonder if Jareth would describe it that way. He's been texting me every couple of hours since I got to the cottage, and I don't really feel like responding. So much pressure. I feel kind of guilty, but I figure he's got to get the picture at some point, right?

We've reached the other side of the lake, but so far there's no sign of a campfire.

"She said it would be easy to see," says Talia. "Maybe they decided not to do it. Maybe we should turn back."

As if in response, a burst of hearty laughter rolls out from behind a spit of trees that juts out into the water in front of us. When we come around the tip of the small peninsula, we see the fire, just ahead.

I lead the way, and Talia hangs back a bit, following a few steps behind.

"Ahoy," I say, raising my arm. The laughter stops as the group turns to look at us, and then a girl waves back.

"Hey!" she yells, standing and walking over to greet us. "Talia, you made it! Come on up!"

"I'm Mark," I say, holding out my hand.

"Hi, Mark," she says, a bit flirtatiously. I wonder if she knows that she's barking up the wrong tree. "Come on up and meet the guys."

"Cool," I say. Talia is still standing behind me, and I turn to look at her, widening my eyes in an attempt to get her to step up beside me.

"The doppelgangers here," says Mariana, pointing toward a pair of grinning guys who are obviously brothers, "are Luke and Randall." They both half stand from their folding chairs and reach out to shake our hands. "Mister Music over there," she says, pointing across the fire toward a stocky, scruffy red-head, who stops strumming on a guitar to give us a little wave, "is Dylan. There should be a few more people showing up in the next little while. Have a seat."

Talia drops onto a log, and I sit next to her and drop my backpack onto the ground in front of me, pulling out a bottle of peach schnapps. "Anyone up for a cocktail?" I ask. "It was this or crème de menthe."

Mariana laughs and takes the bottle, swigging and passing it around. "Darren should be here soon," she says, as if we're supposed to know who that is. "He'll have weed and beer for sure."

"I don't recognize you guys," says Luke. "You must be renters."

"Renters?" I ask.

"There are two kinds of summer people," explains Mariana. "Renters and lifers. Luke and Randall are lifers; their family owns a cottage, and they've been coming here since they were little kids. Dylan and I are renters, which means our folks just rent vacant cottages for the summer."

"Don't forget Darren," says Randall. "He's a townie. Lives here year-round, in a real house."

"It shows, too," laughs Dylan. "He's a real country boy. Hunting and four-wheelers."

"We're kind of complicated, I guess," I say. "We're not really renters, because our grandparents own a cottage. But we're not lifers either, because neither of us has been here for years."

The bottle arrives at Talia, and she passes it to me without taking a sip. "I think I'm going to head back to the cottage," she whispers.

"What?" I say, surprised. "We just got here."

"Yeah," she says. "I know. I'm just not feeling great, to be honest." She stands. "Thanks," she says. "I'll see you guys around."

Before anyone can even respond, she's gone, walking back down to the beach. I glance after her and wonder if I should chase her and see if she's okay, but after her lecture on the walk over here, I'm not really feeling up to that. Besides, the party's just getting started.

"What's with her?" asks Luke.

I shrug. "Beats me." I take a swig from the bottle and pass it along. "She's my cousin, but we barely know each other."

"Mariana?" a voice calls out from the shadows.

Mariana shoves the bottle down and kicks it under my bag before turning around. "Yeah?"

A man emerges from the darkness, the same puppy from before scrabbling around in front of him, tugging at her leash. "Everything all right down here? I'm taking Rosie for a walk."

"Uh, yeah, Dad," says Mariana, and I can hear the eye roll in her voice. "We're fine."

He walks up and stands at the edge of the fire, and looks around at us. "Hi, boys," he says.

"Hey, Mr. Foer," the other three say in unison.

Mariana's dad turns to me. "I don't believe we've met," he says.

I stand, remembering my best suck-up-to-adults manners, and stick out my hand. "Hi," I say. "I'm Mark Vaughn."

"You new to the lake?" he asks me.

"Kind of," I say. "We used to come here when I was a kid. My family has a cottage across the lake. The Tremblays."

His head jerks back in a subtle but unmistakable look of surprise. "The Tremblays," he repeats. "That must make you Janet's boy."

I nod. "You know them?"

"Yes," he says. "I used to, anyway. Well, nice to meet you." He turns back to Mariana. "Remember what I told you about noise."

"Yeah, yeah," she says. "We'll be good."

He briefly glances at me one more time, then turns and walks away, the dog yanking him up toward the road.

He's only been gone for a few seconds when a whistle sounds from the direction of the beach, and everyone turns to stare as a tall and undeniably hunky dude walks up onto the lawn. He's shirtless, carrying a cooler, and has a take-no-prisoners grin.

"Good old Darren," says Mariana. She turns to me and winks. "I hope you're up for a late night."

CHAPTER SIX

TALIA

I head back along the beach, watching the still water, studying the spiky dark lines of the trees against the starlit sky. I don't know what's wrong with me. I hate everything right now, myself most of all. I don't even want to be alone—I just thought I was going to start crying, and I didn't want to look like an idiot in front of a bunch of strangers. I kind of wish Mark had followed me, that he'd actually given a shit about whether I was okay, but I don't think he's a give-a-shit kind of guy.

And now I don't know what to do. If I go back to the cottage, I'll either have to play Trivial Pursuit with Gary, Janet, and Paige, or lie on my bed, staring at the ceiling. Neither of which appeals.

I check my phone just in case Erin has texted me in the few minutes since I last looked.

Nope.

I think Erin's probably done with me. Moved on. Settled into life in the big city. Met someone new by now, for all I know.

Three years is a long time. I was fifteen when I met Erin. I'd just come out as a lesbian, and Erin was identifying as a lesbian, too, back then. We were the only two out lesbians in the school. Ms. Taylor, the art teacher, introduced us to each other. The GSA was Erin's idea, and, as soon as I came out, Ms. Taylor basically roped me into joining. The first two meetings were just me, Erin, and Ms. Taylor, which sounds pathetic but was actually kind of cool. Ms. Taylor was in her late twenties, with this incredible cloud of dark curly hair, and she was totally open about being bisexual. She went to bat with the school administration to get permission for the GSA, and she talked to us about how she refused to be invisible as a queer person just because she was currently living with a man.

At the third GSA meeting, two really sweet gay guys showed up, all blushing and shy but very much together, and at the fourth, we added a goth kid who identified as gender fluid, and three girls who said they were straight but wanted to help out. By that time, Ms. Taylor had pulled back and basically just provided classroom space and snacks, and Erin and I were flirting madly and co-facilitating the meetings. We planned a Halloween dance, which was a GSA thing but open to everyone, and Erin and I went as steampunk time travelers and ended up kissing right on the dance floor, our aviator goggles bumping and our leather-gloved fingers intertwined.

Three years ago this fall. It seems like forever. We're not even the same people we were then.

Erin has always been the one who leads the way, and I just try to keep up. Erin is always so certain about who they are, how they feel, what they want—and I'm just pulled along in their slipstream. I don't even know how I identify now. I mean, I told Mark I'm queer because I don't know what other identity I can claim. I thought I was a lesbian, but can I still identify that way if the person I'm in love with doesn't identify as a girl? I talked about this with Erin, who said maybe I was pansexual, and I went with that for a while. But it doesn't feel true.

How can you say you're pansexual if you've really ever only been attracted to one person? And I'm not attracted to guys, so I can't really be pan, right? Like, I'm definitely not attracted to *all* genders. So maybe I'm bi, because I was attracted to Erin when they identified as a girl, and when they identified as nonbinary. But they were still the same person, so I don't know if that even makes sense.

I check my phone again.

Nothing.

I am pathetic.

I'm almost at the cottage—I can see the lights through the trees—so I slow down, not wanting to face Dad and the others. There's a big ramshackle shed behind the cottage, and I head toward it, wondering if I can maybe sit in there for a bit and write in my journal, which is on my phone. If anyone ever read it, they'd think I was a total mess, because I only write it in when I feel horrible.

I test the door, which is locked, and wander around the back, hoping there might be another way in. Sure enough, there's a side door that is boarded over, but the board is practically hanging by one nail. One good pull and it comes off in my hand, and behind it, the door is unlocked. I slip inside the pitch-dark space, feeling around on the wall for a light switch. Nothing. I pull out my phone and turn on its tiny flashlight, casting the feeble beam around the space. To my surprise, there's a car, and it looks vintage, like something out of an old movie. It must be Grandpa's. By the look of it, it probably hasn't been driven for years. Against one wall, cardboard boxes and Rubbermaid tubs are stacked on wooden shelves.

I bet Dad doesn't even know there's more stuff to deal with out here. Another decade's worth of *National Geographic,* perhaps.

Holding my phone light in front of me, I examine the boxes. They're all neatly labeled: "Spare Bedding and Towels," "Plastic Dish Sets," "Boat Repair," "Fishing Gear," "Magazines," "Memorabilia."

I pull down one of the tubs labeled "Memorabilia" and pry off the lid. It's full of papers—letters, newspaper articles, old photos. My flashlight isn't bright enough for this, so I decide to bring it inside. Maybe there are some old pictures of my family. I don't have a lot of photos from when I was small—I think my mom and dad were too busy fighting, or maybe there just wasn't much about their life that they wanted to record. I was only two when they split up, so it's not like I was horribly scarred by the divorce or anything—I don't even remember them ever being together—but a few photographs would be nice.

Anyway, it'll be an excuse to avoid the family board games.

———————

Paige is the only one in the living room. She's curled up on the couch, with a red-and-white crocheted blanket pulled up to her chin, reading Magnus Chase. She sits up when I drop the heavy tub on the floor in front of her.

"What's that?" she asks.

"Old junk from the shed." I lean backward, stretching my muscles. "Very heavy old junk. Uh . . . what'd you do with your mom and my dad? I thought you'd all be deep into Trivial Pursuit or something."

"Uncle Gary's gone out for a walk. Mom's in her room with a migraine."

"Okay . . . Is that code for they had a big fight?"

Paige nods. "I eavesdropped because I thought maybe one of them would drop a clue, but they just argued about the cottage. I thought this week was going to be fun, but they're not being any fun at all. I wish we never even came here."

"Can I . . ." I point at the couch, she nods, and I sit down beside her. "Want to help me sort through this stuff?"

"What is it?"

"God knows. Probably junk, but there's boxes and boxes of it, and if Grandma's kept it all these years, it seems kind of wrong to let anyone throw it out without even looking through it."

"Maybe there's something in here that will help me figure out why they don't like each other," says Paige. I don't want to rain on her parade, so I just watch as she lifts the lid off the box and pulls out a newspaper article, carefully trimmed. She studies it for a moment, shrugs, and hands it to me.

It's from a Muskoka paper, and the date is carefully written on one corner: "July 17, 1989." Over thirty years ago. I scan the article: it's about a group of summer residents who collected cans of food and cash donations for a food bank in Bracebridge. "Looks like Grandma organized a big fundraiser," I say, studying the grainy photograph: five middle-aged women, all dressed up and smiling for the camera. "Look, that's her there, with this group of women. Wow, she looks a bit like your mom, don't you think?"

But Paige looks like she might cry. "That's so sad."

"What is?"

"Just . . . I don't know. Grandma saving all this stuff, and then what? You get old and no one even wants it."

"Yeah." She's right: it's a totally depressing thought. I look at the picture again. Those women are all in their eighties now.

They could be alone, like Grandma, or in nursing homes, or dead. And there are all these things that they did, things that probably seemed like a big deal at the time, and now no one remembers or cares about any of it. "There are boxes and boxes like this," I say.

"What are we going to do with it?"

I shake my head. "I don't know. I mean, I guess we'll throw it out, right? That's what we're supposed to be doing. Cleaning up. Getting the cottage ready to . . ." Too late I remember that she and Janet don't want the cottage sold.

"We're *supposed* to be spending a week together," Paige says. "And then making a decision as a family. That's what Grandma said she wanted."

"Yeah. Family time." I don't mean it to come out sounding bitter, but it does.

"So much for that," Paige says and gives a world-weary kind of sigh.

"How old are you again?" I say, laughing.

"Ten," she says. "But everyone says I'm an old soul." She reaches into the tub, pulls out a stack of papers, and begins flipping through them. "Hey, here's a picture of my mom. Oh my god, look at her hair! It's huge."

I'm about to reply when my phone vibrates in my hoodie pocket, and I just about jump out of my skin. I pull it out and stare at the screen. It's a text from Erin. "Hang on," I say. "Gotta take this."

I walk away, wanting to be alone with Erin even if they're only on my phone, and I shut myself into my tiny bare room.

Hi Talia. Just got all your texts- phone was dead, sorry. You're in Toronto? Would love to see you.

Friendly but distant. Like I'm an old friend passing through town. I try to strike the same note in my reply. I type, Was in town for my Grandpa's funeral but we're up at the cottage now. Sorry I missed you. How's life in the big city? I re-read what I've written to make sure it doesn't sound clingy or desperate, then I hit send.

It's good. Busy. Working a lot. Sorry about your Grandpa. Are you doing okay?

I try to picture Erin in their room at their brother's place, imagine them cross-legged on their bed in their favorite jeans, phone in hand, sending these messages to me. I stare at the words, trying to read between them: Am I doing okay as in, after my grandpa died? Or am I doing okay as in, without them? I blow out a long breath and type back, I've been better.

There's a long pause—too long—and I wish I could snatch those words back and send something cheerful and non-needy instead.

Then another text: Yeah. Me too. Will you be back in Toronto before you head back west? We should get together.

There's a weird electric jolt in my chest, like when you look down from a ledge and realize it's a longer drop than you thought.

Not really sure what's happening, I type. I'll let you know.

There's a tentative knock on my door. "Talia?"

"Yeah?"

The door opens a couple inches, and half of Paige's face appears in the crack. "I think I may have found something," she says. "Can you come look at this?"

"Now?"

"Yeah. It's kind of weird."

"I'm kind of in the middle of . . ." My phone buzzes. Cool. Gotta go. Ttyl.

So I guess we're done. "Fine," I tell Paige. "Show me."

And then Janet bursts out of her room, waving her phone around above her head. "Where's your father, Talia? Isn't he back yet?" she asks, and she sounds a bit frantic. "And where is Mark?"

"Both out," I say. "What's wrong?"

"Your grandma just called," she says. "I don't think she's doing too well. We need to talk."

CHAPTER SEVEN

MARK

I wake up to light streaming through the window of my tiny room, and the sound of car doors slamming. A few moments later, someone raps on my door.

"Mark!" It's Paige. "Mom says you have to get up! They're going to leave soon!"

I struggle to sit up, noticing for the first time the pounding headache that's starting to spread from my temples down to the rest of my body. I can't remember what time I got back to the cottage. To be honest, I only have a foggy memory of making my way home along the beach, laughing and horsing around with someone.

Darren. I remember now; we walked—or maybe stumbled is more accurate—back along the beach together. Did something happen? No, I'm pretty sure it didn't. But I can remember his bad boy grin, the feeling of his tight muscular arm around my shoulder when he leaned down to pick me up off the beach, where I'd fallen in a fit of laughter. Am I crazy, or do I remember flirting?

"Who's leaving?" I manage to call out.

"Mom and Gary," she calls back. "Grandma's sick, and they're going back to the city."

"What the . . . Okay, I'll be out in a minute." The sound of my voice is so close to my ears that I wince. I reach over and grab my phone from the windowsill. It's almost nine, and I've got a couple of new messages from Jareth.

Am I going to hear from you? Hope you're doing okay . . .

I know I should just ignore him so that he'll eventually get the picture, but I could use a bit of sympathy at the moment, and I know he'll deliver.

Sorry it's been a crazy week and now I'm sick :(Feel like shit.

I don't bother to explain that it's self-inflicted. Sure enough, he responds almost immediately.

Oh no that sucks! got time for a quick call?

Sorry got to head out to do some family stuff. Later?

Okay I'm around all afternoon. xo

I send him a thumbs-up emoji, then somehow manage to swing my legs over the side of the bed. I'm hit right away by a wave of nausea. More of the night is coming back to me, in bits and pieces. The schnapps, which I pretty much polished off by myself. An endless supply of cold cans of beer, passed around from Darren's bottomless cooler.

I pick my T-shirt up off the floor and pull it on, almost gagging at the smell. Campfire and spilled beer. Cigarettes. Was I smoking? Gross.

I wipe my eyes with the back of my hand and walk out into the living room. As I do, Mom comes in from outside and stops when she sees me. I can tell by the look on her face, and the way she's shaking her head at me, that she's seriously pissed off.

"I hope it was worth it," she says, "because you're going to be making up for this for a long time."

"It's no big deal," I say, hoping I don't look as bad as I feel. "I just had a few beers."

"Well, it sure felt like a big deal when I was cleaning vomit off the porch this morning," she says.

"Oh, man," I say, putting my hand to my head and squeezing. "I puked?"

"To be honest, Mark," she says, "I have enough on my mind right now, and I don't want to talk about it. But you can be sure we're not done with this."

"What's wrong with Grandma?" I ask.

"She had a fall," says Mom. "She's in the hospital for some tests, but she isn't doing well."

"Wow," I say, not able to come up with anything better under the circumstances. Fortunately, Paige comes back in from outside.

"Gary's about to leave," she says.

"I thought you were going, too," I say to Mom.

"I am," she says. "We're taking separate cars."

She turns and follows Paige outside, and a moment later I walk out after them.

Gary is standing by his rental with Talia. When she sees me, she turns away and crosses her arms. I am obviously not everyone's favorite person today.

"I won't be far behind you," Mom says to Gary. "I'll meet you at the hospital?"

He nods. "Sounds good." He gives Talia a hug. "You and Paige know the routine?" he asks her, and she nods. He glances at me and winks. "Make sure this vagabond doesn't sit around slacking off all day." He gets into his car and pulls away.

"I don't understand," I say. "Why didn't you just drive together and leave us a car?"

"To tell you the truth, Mark," she says, "Talia doesn't have her license, and I don't feel comfortable leaving the car with you. There's plenty to do around here without you driving off and getting into trouble."

I have a feeling this is just a convenient excuse so that she doesn't have to be stuck with Gary, but I don't push it.

"When will you be back?"

"I'm not sure," she says. "We'll know more once we see how Grandma is doing."

"So basically we're trapped here? What about Pride?"

"What *about* Pride?" she asks, her voice telling me that I'm dangerously close to the edge.

"Toronto Pride is in a few days," I say. "I was hoping I could go."

She laughs. "Fat chance, buddy. I think you've had your fair share of partying for a long time. Anyway, enough of this. The village is just a short walk around the lake, and Talia has grocery money. The list of chores is on the fridge, and I'll be looking for a report to make sure you did your fair share, and then some, do you understand?"

I nod.

"Okay, guys," she says, her voice softening. "Thank you for sticking around to help out. You'll have a better time here than in the city, sitting around the hospital with us." She gives Paige a hug, and then Talia. Then, after a brief pause, she hugs me, too. "Look after your sister, and behave yourself, Mark."

"Yeah," I say. "I will."

After Mom pulls out of the driveway, the three of us stand there looking at each other.

"Well, I guess we should get to work," says Talia after a moment.

I groan. "This is going to suck."

"Well, it isn't going to be a whole lot of fun for me either," says Talia.

"At least you aren't sick," I say.

"You don't get sympathy for a hangover," she says.

"You have a hangover?" Paige asks, her eyes wide.

"It's one of the perks of being a grown-up," I say. "I'm going to have a nap on the deck. I'll help when I wake up, I promise."

I don't have the energy to discuss it any longer, so I somehow drag my ass around to the deck and collapse into a lounge chair. I sleep—or *half*-sleep—for a couple of hours or so, semiconsciously aware that Talia and Paige are bustling about like a couple of worker bees. I know I should be helping, but I feel so gross that the thought of moving makes me even weaker.

"Wake up," a voice says, and I jerk awake. I must have fallen asleep after all. I sit up, rubbing my eyes, and squint up at Paige, who is standing beside me holding a plate with a sandwich.

"You want some lunch?" she asks.

I realize I'm ravenous, and I take the plate gratefully. "What is it?"

"It's a veggie sandwich," she says.

"Veggie," I repeat. "Oh boy, my favorite."

"Talia made them," she says. "They're actually really good. She made hummus from scratch."

I take a bite. It really *is* good. I inhale the rest of the sandwich, and then belch. Paige is sitting on a chair across from me, watching me intently.

"Do you still have a hangover?" she asks.

I pause, taking stock. "No," I say. "I think it's gone, thank god."

"Mom says a hangover is a punishment for acting like a dummy," she says.

"She's not wrong," I say, rising from the lounge chair and stretching. "Stick to milkshakes, kid."

I take the plate into the kitchen and drop it in the sink. Talia is in the living area, in the corner on her hands and knees, scrubbing behind a radiator.

"Hey, Cinderella," I say. "Thanks for the sandwich; it was awesome."

She looks up at me, and I can tell that she's working hard to hold back her disapproval.

"You're welcome," she says. She goes back to scrubbing, but when she realizes I'm still hovering, she sighs and stands, pulling off her rubber gloves.

"How was the party?" she asks.

"It was fun," I say. "The parts I remember, anyway."

She doesn't match my smile. "Drinking until you black out is incredibly stupid, you know. People die doing that. You could have gotten alcohol poisoning or fallen in the lake on your way home."

"I know, I know," I say. I hold up a hand. "Scout's honor, I don't usually act that way. I mean, I'll have a couple of beers once in a while, but I generally try to avoid the calories. Besides, I had an escort home."

"Mariana?" she asks.

"No. Darren. He showed up not long after you left. You might have passed him on the beach; he lives just a few cottages down from us."

"The guy with no shirt and a cooler?" she asks.

"That's the one." I want her to ask me more, but she doesn't seem interested. "Anyway, it was fun, and he's cute, and that's the story so far. You left pretty quick. Everything okay?"

She shrugs. "Yeah, I know it was weird of me to bolt like that, but I'm not really comfortable around that kind of party. You know, 'cool kids.' Not my scene."

"They're just people," I say. "They're no cooler than either of us. They're actually really nice. Mariana was disappointed you didn't stick around. She said she gets bored of hanging out with dudes all the time."

"I guess I just needed some time to myself," she says. "After the funeral, and our parents fighting, and Erin . . ." She trails off.

"I totally get it," I say. "It's been a shitty week all around. Anyway, I have an idea. I know there are a million jobs to do, and I promise I'll pitch in, but first I think the three of us should take a little break for a couple of hours."

She looks at me skeptically. "What do you have in mind?"

"I was just thinking maybe we should stroll down and check out the dock," I say. "You know, to test its structural integrity."

Like the cottage, the beach hasn't changed since I was a kid. The same red paint on the dock, the same fire pit beside the water.

"Oh wow," I say, looking into the tangle of weeds and bushes on the far edge of the little gravel beach. "Come check this out."

They come over and peer at the old canoe, tipped upside down with a tarp tied tightly over it.

"Grandpa's canoe," says Talia.

A hush of sadness falls over us, the opposite of what I was going for.

"Did you see him much?" Talia asks. "I mean, after we stopped coming to the cottage?"

I shake my head. "In Toronto, a couple times. I guess I was twelve and again at maybe fourteen? But just short visits. Then they both came east last Christmas." I hadn't thought I'd never see Grandpa again, though. I'd have made more time for him if I'd known that.

"I remember being out on the lake with him. Like, I have really vivid memories. He used to whistle while he paddled . . ." She stares at the canoe. "It's kind of sad to see it now. Left behind."

"We'll take it out!" I say, trying to cut through the somber mood.

"Now?" asks Paige.

"No, not now," I say. "We'll have to dig out lifejackets and stuff, but later this week. For now, we'll have to make do with swimming!"

As Paige and Talia make their way slowly into the water from the beach, I jump in from the dock. As I slip through the surface of the water, the shock of the chill gives me an odd sensation, as if a switch has been flipped. When I surface, kicking my way up from the seaweed and mud at the bottom, I feel almost like a different person. Or, the same person maybe, just younger, newer.

"It's awesome!" I yell. "Quit wasting time and get in!"

The lake is like a bath that washes away the past ten years of my life. My hangover disappears, the endless tickle of guilt that I've been feeling about Jareth recedes, and I'm left amazed at how much I feel like a kid again. The top few inches of water are warm and inviting, but when I stop to tread water, my feet sink down into icy hidden pockets, leaving me shivering and exhilarated.

When I'm this low, my head sticking just above the surface, the cottages on the opposite side of the lake disappear, and all I can see is an endless tree-topped shoreline. It's almost possible to imagine that we're the only people here, that the distant sounds of screaming kids are just our own voices echoing back at us from years ago.

We spend an hour in the lake, splashing and swimming and laughing. By the time we walk back up to the cottage, collapsing into lounge chairs to dry off in the sun, it's like things have shifted back in the right direction. Talia seems a lot happier, and Paige is beside herself with excitement.

"I wish I'd been able to spend my summers here, like you guys," she says. "It's so amazing."

I smile at Talia, and she smiles back. I'm glad that things have fallen back into this groove.

"Who is Frank?" asks Paige.

"Who?" Talia and I both look at her, confused.

"Frank," she says again. "I found this . . . this *thing* in one of the boxes from the shed. Hang on, I'll show you." She gets up from her chair and goes into the cottage.

"The shed?" I ask Talia.

"I was out there last night," she says. "There are dozens of boxes of old stuff. An old car, too."

"A car?" I ask, my interest piqued. "What kind?"

She shrugs. "Not sure. It's ancient, though. I doubt it works."

Paige comes back out and hands me a long, narrow photo album. Inside the front cover, in careful calligraphy, someone has written, *Bracebridge Summer Days: Janet, Gary, and Frank, the "honorary Tremblay."*

We go through the photos, one after the other. Each page is labeled with a year, beginning in 1978, and a photograph of Mom and Gary, beginning when they were little kids and progressing through the years. In each photo, they're posed at the end of the dock, in the exact same positions. Mom in the middle, Gary to her right, and on Mom's left, another cheeky, smiling boy. Their arms are draped around each other, and there are big grins on their faces.

"I guess that's Frank," says Talia, pointing to the third kid.

We flip through the book, watching them grow up, year after year. The last page is from 1992, and the three of them are almost young adults, their wide, childish grins replaced by more laid-back teenage smiles.

"It's sad to see them so happy," says Talia. "They look like they were close."

I'm staring at the picture of teenage Frank. I can't put my finger on it, but he looks vaguely familiar, although I'm sure I've never heard of him.

"Who is he?" asks Paige again.

We both shake our heads.

"Looks like it was just some friend of theirs," says Talia. "I'm sure it doesn't mean anything."

"But it has to mean something!" says Paige. "It even says 'honorary Tremblay' right here!" She jabs her finger against the cover. "Why wouldn't we have ever heard about him if he was basically like their brother? That makes him, like, our uncle!"

"People lose touch all the time, Paige," I say.

"Well, I'm going to find out who Frank was," she says, grabbing the book and stomping back into the cottage.

The thing is, it *is* kind of weird that none of us have ever heard of Frank in all these years.

CHAPTER EIGHT

TALIA

It's a warm sunny morning, the sky a clear blue, the sun reflecting off the lake. On a day like this, it should be impossible to be in a bad mood. I'm managing, though. Three reasons: One, I texted Erin last night and stupidly said how much I missed them, and they didn't reply. Two, Mark is off somewhere with Darren, being no help at all. And, three, Paige and I are tackling the linen cupboard, and it is apparently bottomless.

"Why would anyone have so many towels?" Paige asks. "You could use, like, three a day and still go a year without doing laundry."

I tie off another garbage bag, write "TOWELS" on a piece of masking tape, and stick it on. "I have absolutely no idea. I guess they just accumulated." I eye the stacks. "Or reproduced."

She puts her hands on her hips and stares at the cupboard. "You know what it reminds me of?"

"What?"

"One of those magic trick chests where the magician keeps pulling stuff out, scarves and rabbits and whatever, and it never ever gets empty."

I snort a laugh. "Yeah, that's about right."

"What are we going to do with all this stuff?" she asks. "I mean, if Grandma does decide to sell the cottage? It's all perfectly good, but there's no way she needs all this stuff."

I picture Grandma's tiny, overstuffed condo. "Maybe we can donate it somewhere." I stand and stretch, pushing my hands against my lower back. "You're right, though. We need to make sure it doesn't end up in a landfill."

"Oh! We should have a garage sale," Paige says. "That'd be so much fun."

I can't think of anything I'd rather do less. All I want is to get this done, and get back to Toronto with time to see Erin before Dad and I have to head back west. I'm just opening my mouth to answer when an ear-splitting horn shatters the quiet.

"What was THAT?" Paige is on her feet and flying out the door, and I follow. From the deck, we can hear laughter.

"Mark and Darren," I say. "They must be in the shed. I bet that's the horn from Grandpa's old car." I can't help feeling annoyed: that car was obviously precious to Grandpa, and they shouldn't be messing around with it. Plus, it's been two days since our parents left, and in that time, Mark has done precisely nothing to help get the cottage in order. He's unbelievable.

Apparently, no one has ever called him on his shit, because when I try to, he acts totally hurt and offended, and I end up feeling like the world's most uptight person.

"Let's go see," Paige says.

"Hold on," I say, but she's already flying down the path, so I follow.

Inside the shed, Mark and Darren have taken the canvas cover off the car and are sitting in the front seats, laughing their heads off.

"What are you guys doing?" Paige asks. "Does the car work? How old is it? It looks like a car from an old action movie."

She's right, it totally does: long, low, and mustard yellow with a black racing stripe.

"Ford Mustang," Darren says. He's tall, broad-shouldered, with sandy blond hair. His tanned arms and face are dark against his white T-shirt, and he's got a lazy kind of grin. "1970. Pretty sweet, huh?"

I shrug. "Pretty irrelevant, actually."

"Talia . . ." Mark gets out of the driver's seat and holds his hands out, palms up, like he's reaching out to me. "I know I said I'd help today, but . . ."

"But instead you decided to do your own thing and leave me to do the work? Kind of like you did yesterday? Oh, and to babysit your sister, too?"

I glance at Paige, who looks like I just slapped her, and I wish I could take back those last words. "Not that I mind that part," I say hastily. "She's a huge help."

"Look, I'm sorry," Mark says. "But the thing is, this car is kind of part of the cottage, right? And if it has to be sold, well, Grandma would probably get a lot more money for it if Darren and I can get it running. So we thought we could do a little work on it."

I can just imagine. "Do you either of you even know anything about cars? Or were you just planning to sit in it and drink beer all afternoon?"

"Hey," Darren says, looking hurt. "My dad's a mechanic. I've worked in his shop since I was twelve."

Mark gives me a smug look. "So . . . okay?"

"Whatever," I say, and turn to walk away.

"Talia . . . Don't be mad," he says.

I ignore him. Paige runs up behind me as we walk, and grabs my hand. "I'll help you," she says. "Don't worry."

"I know," I say. "That's not the point."

"What is the point?"

"Forget it," I say. "Let's take a break. Want to go get ice cream?"

"Sure!"

"There's a great place that does soft serve with chocolate dip, if it's still there," I say. "It's one of the things I remember about the cottage. Mark and I used to walk there together, right up until we were your age."

"When our families stopped coming to the cottage," Paige says, following me up the wooden steps to the cottage door. "Why did they?"

I shrug. "Dad says we just got busy with other things, but I think your mom and my dad had a fight." I step inside, grab my phone—still no new texts—and slide it into the pocket of my cargo shorts. "Or maybe they argued with Grandma? I don't know. My dad won't talk about it."

"What about your mom?"

I step into the kitchen and pull a twenty-dollar bill from the envelope of grocery money. "My parents split up when I was a toddler," I say. "I've always lived with my dad."

"You don't see your mom?"

"I see her," I say, "but she lives a two-hour drive away, so not that much." As little as possible, actually. Especially since she got converted by some door-to-door evangelist type. I'm not even out to her, because why bother? I don't need a lecture on sin from my own mother. "Anyway, she wouldn't know anything about this."

Paige picks up her hoodie off the couch. Lying beside it is the photo album—the one with all the photos of Dad, Janet, and Frank (the honorary Tremblay).

"Hey," I say, pointing. "Let's bring that. Maybe someone at the ice cream shop will be able to tell us who the mystery guy is."

She brightens. "Detective work!"

"Exactly."

It's a half-hour walk into the village, along a dirt road that runs parallel to the lake for a way and then curves off through the woods. Paige chatters for a few minutes, and then we fall into an amiable silence, listening to the birds and the rustle of the breeze through the leaves of the tall maples. It's peaceful here, and as Paige points out, the air "smells like green things."

The village isn't really a village at all, just a cluster of small houses, a tiny grocery store, a gas station, a real estate office that also sells horse-riding treks, and a few other little businesses. The ice cream shop is still there, and it looks exactly as I remembered it: blue and yellow paint and a kitschy country-style aesthetic. A wooden sandwich board sign out front says *MUSKOKA'S BEST ICE CREAM!!!*

"It looks like it's been here forever," Paige whispers. "I bet they'll know Frank."

"Yeah, for sure," I say. "Frank and your mom and my dad probably came here together all the time." But when we step inside, I realize we're out of luck: The guy behind the counter looks younger than I am. "Hi," he says, flashing a mouthful of braces. "Can I help you?"

"Want a chocolate dip?" I ask Paige, who nods. I slide the twenty across the counter. "Two chocolate dip cones, then. Thanks."

We watch him work the machine, swirling creamy vanilla ice cream into one cone and then another. "Are you going to ask him?" Paige asks, nudging me with the poky corner of the photo album.

I shrug. "No point."

She glares at me and flips the photo album onto the counter. "Hey, can I ask you a question?"

Ice Cream Guy hands her a cone and passes the other one to me. "Sure, what's up?"

She opens the album to the last page: a photo of our parents and Frank looking about my age. "Do you know who this is?" she asks, her fingertip jabbing Frank's chest.

He shakes his head. "Sorry. I've only been here a year. You should ask Mr. Ward; he knows everything."

Paige whips out a pen and notebook that I had no idea she had. "Mister . . . Ward," she says, writing it down. "And can you tell me his whereabouts?"

I hold back my laughter—she'll pull out a magnifying glass in a minute, or start dusting the glass counter for fingerprints.

"He owns the store," Ice Cream Guy tells her. "But he's not here much." He grins, and his cheeks turn pink. "He leaves me in charge when he's not around."

I'm about to ask him when Mr. Ward will be back when my phone vibrates in my pocket and I jump like I just got an electric shock. "Hang on," I say to Paige. "I just have to . . ." I take a few steps away and turn my back before checking the screen.

It's Erin. I really miss you too. I think we should talk.

The flood of relief is an actual physical thing, a warmth rushing through every vein, every muscle, every cell in my body. I drop into one of the white enamel chairs and resist the urge to kiss my phone.

Okay, yes. Me too, I type. My mind is racing. *We should talk* could mean so many things. *We should talk about getting back together? We should talk about moving on? We should talk about . . .*

Been doing a lot of thinking. Better to talk in person though. Any chance of you coming down to Toronto? Just for a day, even? Or overnight?

I blow out a long, unsteady breath. It's not that far. Two and a half hours' drive. There's probably a bus I could take.

"Your ice cream is melting," Paige says, appearing in front of me.

I look down. Ice cream is dripping down the side of my cone and I catch it with my tongue before it reaches my hand. "Oops."

"Is everything okay?" Paige eyes my phone. "Is Grandma . . ."

"She's fine." I shake my head. "I mean, I don't know. I wasn't talking to Dad. Just a friend." I read over Erin's last message and type quickly, Maybe. I have to call my dad. I'll let you know.

I don't see why my dad should object. I mean, he's in Toronto himself.

And surely Mark can look after his own sister for a day or two.

CHAPTER NINE

MARK

Working on the Mustang is really kind of cool. For one thing, I've always liked anything mechanical. In fact, I've been thinking about going into engineering after I graduate. There's something extra cool about this hands-on stuff, and Darren really seems to know what he's doing.

If I'm being honest, that's the main reason working on the car is so rewarding. Darren is totally into it, and I'm into hanging out with him.

We find some old tools under the workbench, and he pops the hood and starts poking around.

It's hot in the shed, and before long, Darren has taken his shirt off and tossed it over the back of an old stacking chair. This guy likes to take his shirt off; he's like the Matthew McConaughey of Muskoka. I try not to stare, but it's difficult.

"Man, it's kind of crazy that your Grandpa just kept this car here the whole time," he says as he reaches deep into the car's innards and twists a wrench. "She's in pretty good shape. I wonder if he's had it long."

"I don't remember it from when I was a kid," I say. "But maybe it was here the whole time. Who knows? I was paying more attention to the beach and board games back then."

Darren stands up and drops the hood closed. He points to the driver's-side door. "You mind?"

"Go for it."

I climb into the passenger seat and watch as Darren adjusts his seat and runs his hand over the steering wheel and the dash.

"Man, this is a beautiful car." He turns the key in the ignition, and the engine wheezes and chokes a little bit, but doesn't turn over.

"That sucks," I say.

"Don't worry. We'll get her back up and running." He turns around and glances into the backseat, then turns to me, grinning. "Lots of room back there. A guy could make some serious progress in a backseat like that, if you catch my drift." He winks at me.

"Oh, I catch your drift," I say, trying to sound cool, although my mouth has gone dry. Is he flirting with me?

"Hey!"

We both turn to the door, where Paige is standing against the glare from outside. I grit my teeth, trying not to curse her for interrupting—whatever this is. We climb out of the car, and

76

I'm kind of disappointed when Darren grabs his shirt and pulls it back on.

"What's going on, Paige?" I ask.

"Guess what?" she asks. She comes into the shed and pulls a notebook out of her back pocket. "I found a clue."

"A clue?" asks Darren. "You out solving mysteries or something?"

"Just one mystery," says Paige. "The mystery of the missing brother."

Darren's eyebrows lift, surprised. "That does sound like kind of a big mystery. How do you lose a brother?"

"It's not really a brother," I explain. "Just some kid who used to hang out with our mom and Talia's dad. I guess he isn't a kid anymore, since this was like a million years ago, in the nineties."

"So Talia and I got ice cream in town," says Paige, "and the kid who was working said that the man who owns the ice cream shop might know who he was."

"Mr. Ward?" asks Darren.

"That's him!" says Paige. "You know him?"

"Yeah, for sure," says Darren. "Everyone knows Mr. Ward. He owns, like, half the businesses around here."

"Really?" asks Paige. "Like what else?"

"Well," says Darren. "He and his wife operate a bed and breakfast; it's a big fancy house on the main drag, with a nice garden. He's usually at the marina, though. He owns the boat rental place."

Paige looks at me. "Can we go?" she asks. "Please?"

"Now?" I ask. "You just got back from town."

"I don't care," she says. "This is important."

"I'm kind of busy, Paige," I say, gesturing toward the car. "Maybe tomorrow."

"If you don't take me to the marina, I'll text Mom and tell her you're neglecting me," she says.

I stare at her, openmouthed. Darren laughs.

"This girl does not play softball," he says. "Listen, Mark, I gotta get out of here anyway. Maybe I can swing back around tomorrow and we can mess around with this beast some more." He smacks the hood of the car with the palm of his hand.

"That sounds great," I say. "I'll be around all day."

"Cool, man," says Darren. "Take it easy."

I wave after him as he takes off, then I turn to glare at Paige.

"You're blackmailing me?" I ask.

"You're letting Talia do all the work," she says. "It's not fair. You come help me with this and I won't bug you tomorrow. I'll distract Talia, too, so she doesn't feel like she's pulling your weight."

"When did you become such a hardcore negotiator?" I ask her.

She shrugs. "I is who I is."

"Fine," I say. "Let's go."

Talia is sitting on the porch, staring at her phone, as we cross the yard.

"We're going sleuthing," I say. "You wanna come?"

She shakes her head. "No. I might call my father. I was wondering—I just thought maybe we should check in and see how Grandma is doing."

"Good idea," I say. "We won't be long."

As we walk up the drive toward the road, I glance back. Talia is still looking at her phone but not making a call.

"Mark?" asks Paige. "If you're boyfriends with Jareth, don't you think it's a bad idea to flirt with Darren?"

"Um, what are you talking about?" I ask. "I'm not flirting with Darren."

"Yeah, right," she says.

"Okay, fine," I say, "but flirting isn't a big deal. Besides, Jareth isn't really my boyfriend anymore."

"Did you guys break up?"

"Not exactly," I say. "I mean, we're just on, like, a summer break."

"Huh." She considers this. "I didn't know that was a thing."

I can tell she has a hundred more questions, so I'm thrilled when we turn a corner and come across Mariana being dragged down the road by Rosie.

"Hey!" she says, raising a hand to us. "I was just coming to see what you guys were up to."

We stop and Paige crouches to play with the puppy.

"We're on our way into town," I say. "Paige is on a very important mission. Talia's back at the cottage, though. Maybe you can try to cheer her up. I'm not really her favorite person right now."

"Why not?" asks Mariana.

"Mark would rather flirt with boys than help out around the cottage," says Paige, standing up. "He and Jareth are on a summer break."

"I see," says Mariana. The look on her face confirms my suspicion that she hadn't figured out I was gay. She recovers quickly, though, and smiles at me. "Any boys in particular?"

"He's been fixing a car with Darren," says Paige.

"What is going on with you?" I ask Paige. "Have you decided to just start blurting out everything that comes into your head?"

"Darren?" asks Mariana.

"He's helping me fix our grandpa's old car," I say. "Paige's overactive imagination is just filling in some blanks, apparently."

"Ewww," says Paige, pointing. Rosie is circling in the weeds on the side of the road, obviously preparing to poop.

"This seems like a good time to get going," I say.

Mariana laughs, pulling a bag out of her pocket. "I don't blame you. Maybe I will stop and visit Talia. You don't think she'll mind?"

"I think she could use some company," I say. "If you guys become best friends, please tell her that her cousin Mark isn't as much of a jerk as she thinks."

"I'll do my best," says Mariana. "I was actually thinking that you guys could come over for a barbecue sometime this week. You too, Paige. My dad's a great cook, and he likes to show it off. Besides, he was asking me all about you."

"Me?" I ask, surprised.

"Yeah," she says. "I guess you made an impression."

"Sounds cool," I say. "We'd be into that."

We leave Mariana to deal with Rosie's mess and continue on our way.

The marina is pretty busy, with locals coming in and out of the boat shop. Offshore, there's a group of small day sailers bobbing about, crewed by kids. It looks like they're racing.

"That looks fun," says Paige. "I wish we could come here and do that."

"You could go sailing in Halifax," I say. "There's tons of sailing back home."

"I want to do it here," she says with a stubborn lift of her chin. "Look, there's the boat rental place."

I turn and see that she's pointing to a small, neatly painted cottage on the edge of the marina. A sign above the door reads *Ward's Boat Rental.*

Paige immediately starts marching toward it, and I hustle to keep up with her. A few older men are sitting outside in Muskoka chairs. Paige walks right up to them.

"Is one of you Mr. Ward?" she asks.

One of the men pushes his sunglasses down to the end of his nose and peers over them at her.

"That would be me," he says. "How can I help you, young lady?"

"I was talking to the guy who works at your ice cream store this morning," she says. "He told me you might be able to help me out with something." She pulls the photo album out of her backpack and flips to the most recent picture of Mom and Gary and Frank. She hands it across to him. After a moment, he smiles with recognition.

"Janet Tremblay," he says, nodding.

"You know her?" asks Paige, clearly excited. "She's our mom!"

He looks up at us and squints. "I can definitely see the resemblance," he says. "Janet worked for me, as a matter of fact. Two summers at the ice cream shop. Or maybe one summer, I can't quite remember."

"Do you remember the other guy?" I ask. "This one, I mean?" I point. Despite myself, I'm starting to get excited that we might be close to solving the mystery.

"Sure," he says. "Frank. He was good buddies with your mom and your Uncle Gary. Frank and Gary used to come hang out at the shop when your mother was working."

"Do you remember his last name?" I ask.

He frowns and shakes his head. "Sorry, kids. Only reason I knew your mother's last name is because she worked for me. So many people come in and out of this area every summer, I'm lucky if I know their first names."

He looks back at the photo album, and then at Paige. "If you're Janet's daughter, why don't you just ask her?"

Paige wrinkles her nose. "She's in Toronto. Visiting my grandma in the hospital."

"Sorry to hear that," Mr. Ward says. "Well, you give her my best."

CHAPTER TEN

TALIA

I've tried about a dozen ways of asking my dad if I can go down to Toronto for a day or two . . . but only in my head. Like, I could say I'm really worried about Grandma and want to see her, or I could say I have a toothache—though I guess there are dentists closer than Toronto.

I think honesty might actually work best: I could just tell him that I need to see Erin. I mean, he's fond of Erin. And the two of us basically spent every minute together until about two weeks ago, so he should understand that we'd be missing each other like crazy.

Still, even within the honesty approach, there are different strategies. I could go with casual, like it's nothing major, just a little day trip to the city, and hope that he agrees: *yeah, sure, why not, no big deal.* Or I could go with more emotionally desperate in the hope that he won't say no if he sees how much it matters to me. I could even, if I need to, admit that Erin and I are having some problems.

I blow out a long breath, staring at my phone. Then I make the call.

It rings a few times, but he picks up just before it goes to voicemail, sounding out of breath. "Hello?"

"Dad, hi."

"Is everything okay?"

"Yes, fine. How's Grandma?"

"She's doing okay," he says. "A few bruises from the fall, but nothing broken, luckily."

"Why did she fall, though?"

"She says she got dizzy. Her doctor thinks she was overdoing things, and it caught up with her."

"That's good, right?" I ask. "I mean, it sounds like there's nothing seriously wrong?"

"It's good for now, but the big question is, what happens next? He wants to keep her in the hospital for a few days, just to monitor her. Anyway, we'll have to wait and see. How are things at the cottage?"

"Good. So, uh, I was thinking. Erin's invited me to come down to Toronto for a day or two, so maybe I could take a day or two off and head down to the city?"

He sounds taken aback. "Right now? In the middle of all this?"

"Well, yeah."

"Look, I need you to stay and help out. With Grandma's current condition, I think even Janet is acknowledging that the cottage is going to have to be sold."

"Yeah, but not urgently," I say. "I mean, I'm talking about one day. Besides, I've done lots already. Unlike Mark—"

"Hang on," he says. I can hear him talking to someone else but can't make out his words. "I'll call you back, Talia."

And he disconnects.

Crap.

I'm still staring at my phone when I hear someone call my name. I look up and see Mariana walking toward me, her puppy bounding along at her side, ears flapping like little wings.

"Hi, Mariana," I say, holding out a hand for the dog to sniff. "It's Rosie, right?"

"Yeah. Can I . . ." She gestures to the step I'm sitting on, and I nod.

She drops down to sit beside me. "I just saw Mark and his little sister," she says. "And, uh . . ."

I look at her. "What?"

"Um, I think his sister just kind of outed him, maybe?" Her cheeks flush pink. "Maybe I misunderstood, but I think she said something about him chasing boys."

"Yeah. I guess maybe I should've told you?"

"No, no. I mean, yeah, it would've been good to know, but I shouldn't have assumed he was straight, right?"

"True," I say. "You shouldn't."

She looks a bit taken aback, and I wonder if she's hastily revising any assumptions she's made about me. "Anyway, his sister also said he was hanging out with Darren."

"Yeah." I point at the shed. "There's this old car in there that they're fixing up. Or pretending to fix up. I think they just sit in it, drinking beer."

"Darren's a decent mechanic," Mariana says. "They'll probably get it running. But . . ." She leans forward and pries a stone out of Rosie's mouth. "No, puppy. Don't chew that."

"But what?"

She shifts, turning to face me. "Darren's fun and he's good looking. But he can be kind of an asshole."

"Sounds like a match made in heaven," I say a little bitterly.

She looks shocked. "Mark seems so nice . . ."

I sigh. "He is. He is nice. Just really, really clueless sometimes."

She nods. "Well, you might want to give him a heads-up about Darren. That he's not always the great guy he wants everyone to think he is."

"That'll go over well," I say. "He already thinks I exist mainly to get in the way of him having a good time."

Mariana laughs. "Hey, speaking of good times . . . You want to come to a barbecue at my place? Tomorrow, maybe? Or the next day? Or . . . well, any day, really. It's not like we have any plans."

I'm just opening my mouth to answer when my phone rings. I hold up a finger. "One sec."

It's Dad. "Talia, hi." Brisk and businesslike. "I talked to Janet, and I think we'd both feel better if you stayed at the cottage. Apparently, Mark came home drunk a few nights ago . . ."

"And puked all over the porch, yeah, I remember."

"Yes. Anyway." He clears his throat. "We'd rather you were there as well, to keep an eye on things."

"So I'm babysitting Mark as well as Paige? That is so unfair, Dad. I'm basically being punished for being responsible."

"You are not being punished, Talia. And you're not babysitting. You are helping out your family during an emergency situation, and I'd like you to do that without making a fuss."

"But Dad. It's—"

"Not now, Talia. I have to go. Grandma's doctor wants to talk to me and Janet, and—"

"One day," I say. "That's all. I could go and come back—"

"Enough," he snaps. "Seriously, Talia. And I really do have to go. Please. Just step up, all right?"

I hang up without even saying goodbye. My heart is racing. Maybe it's not fair to blame this all on Mark, but I am so pissed off at him right now.

"Everything okay?" Mariana asks.

"Not really," I say. I'll have to text Erin and say it's not looking hopeful.

"I'm sorry." Mariana pushes her sunglasses up on her forehead and studies me with those big dark eyes. "I don't want to be nosy, but if you want to talk about it . . ."

I shake my head and blow out a long sigh. Her eyelashes are the longest I've ever seen. Compared with her, I barely even *have* eyelashes. "On the plus side," I say, "it sounds like I'm free for a barbecue tomorrow."

After Mariana leaves, I head into the cottage and text Erin. Hey.

I wait a moment but there's no reply.

Doesn't look like I'll be able to come down to Toronto. I stare at the words, then delete them. I don't really think Dad will change his mind, but I'm not admitting defeat yet.

Then it occurs to me: the busses run both ways. Maybe Erin could come up here, stay at the cottage for a few days.

Not sure I'll be able to come to Toronto, I type, but why don't you come up here? It's just me and my cousins. Dad's away.

Footsteps thump up the front steps, the cottage door bangs open, and Paige comes flying through. "Talia, GUESS WHAT?!"

I stick my phone in my pocket. "What?"

"We got more information! My mom worked at the ice cream shop."

"Cool." It's weird thinking of our parents being our age. "Did you find out more about Frank?"

She shakes her head. "Not really. Mr. Ward remembered him, but only his first name and we already knew that." She points at my pocket. "Were you on the phone? Who were you talking to?"

"Nosy much?"

She ignores that. I sigh. "Erin. My . . . friend."

Her eyes widen. "Boyfriend?"

I decide to ignore the question of whether we're a couple, since I'm not too sure myself. "Erin's not really a boy or a girl."

"That's not true. You have to be one or the other," Paige explains, all serious. Like this might be something I'm not aware of and she's helping me out by explaining it like I'm six.

"Lots of people think that, but gender is really way more complicated," I say. "And some people, like Erin, just aren't one or the other."

She looks at me, forehead furrowed.

Okay, time for Gender 101. "So the idea of boys and girls, men and women—that's a binary system," I explain. "Either/or, right?"

"Right. One or the other. Like I said."

"But the thing is, that whole binary system leaves out lots of people. Like Erin. They're nonbinary."

"Like, in between?"

"Yeah, sort of. Maybe." I'm not sure how to explain this to a ten-year-old without totally oversimplifying, but Paige is a smart kid, so I plow on. "Or just . . . I don't know exactly. Erin says they're somewhere in between, but maybe it's not exactly like being in between for everyone who's nonbinary. But yeah, Erin says sometimes they feel more like a boy and sometimes more like a girl, but mostly they just feel like a person who isn't either of those."

"Oh!" Paige has, apparently, moved on. "The other thing is, we saw the girl with the puppy."

"I know. Mariana. She came by here and invited us to a barbecue." I frown at her. "You know, you really shouldn't tell people Mark's gay."

"I didn't."

"You told Mariana he was chasing boys . . ."

"Because he is." Her lower lip sticks out a little. "So why shouldn't I say that?"

I shrug. I don't think people should out other people, but at the same time, it's kind of cool that it's such a nonissue to her. "I guess as long as he doesn't care, then it's cool."

My phone buzzes in my pocket and I pull it out. It's Erin: I have to work the next three days. I have the weekend off but it's Pride, so . . .

Right. Why hang out with me when you could hang out with a million queer strangers who are probably all way cooler and way more fun?

CHAPTER ELEVEN

MARK

Darren and I spend most of the morning working on the car. By the time we break for lunch, the engine is actually turning over.

"You're amazing," I tell him as he wipes sweat off his face with a rag.

He laughs. "It helps to have an old man who's handy with a monkey wrench." He pulls his phone out of his pocket and glances at it. "Shit. I've gotta bail. I'm getting paid to help move some furniture this afternoon."

"Cool," I say. "You'll stop by tomorrow?"

"Sure," he says. "Maybe we can take her for a test drive, bring her into town, and see what she's good for."

I think back to his comment about the backseat and wonder if that's what he's referring to now.

"Sounds perfect," I say, trying to strike a balance between flirty and not-too-flirty. The truth is, I'm not thrilled about the idea of taking Grandpa's car away from the cottage, but the thought of the two of us alone for a few hours makes it worth the risk.

In the afternoon, Paige and I go for a swim. She's super excited about the barbecue, and I'm looking forward to it, too. Hanging out at Mariana's sounds like a better option than sitting on the deck watching Talia stare at her phone and mope.

When we walk back up from the lake to the cottage, however, she isn't moping at all. Inside, she's moving smoothly around the kitchen, chopping and whisking and grating. She actually seems to be enjoying herself.

"What are you making?" Paige asks her.

"Just a salad to bring to Mariana's," she says. "We had a bunch of stuff in the fridge that needed to be used."

"You mind if I put some music on?" I ask her. She nods vaguely, and I spend a few minutes skimming through my playlists, trying to choose something that everyone can enjoy.

"Ah ha," I say, pressing play. As music fills the cottage, I grab Paige by the hand, pulling her up off the couch.

"What is this?" she asks.

"Are you kidding me?" I ask. "It's 'Modern Love.' David Bowie. Don't you know Bowie?"

She shakes her head and grimaces at me as I begin to dance, but I know that Paige is unable to resist, and, sure enough, in a matter of moments she's following me around the living room, imitating my bad attempt at the robot.

I glance toward the kitchen, pleased to see that Talia is actually bobbing her head in time to the music as she stretches plastic wrap over the top of the salad bowl.

"Bowie was a pioneer," I say, projecting my voice to make sure Talia hears me. "He was androgynous before it was cool."

"What does *androgynous* mean?" Paige asks as she shimmies across the room.

"It kind of means blurring the line between what's feminine and what's masculine," I say.

"Oh," she says, "like nonbinary."

"Not exactly," I say, surprised, "but close." I turn to call into the kitchen. "Hey, Talia! Come dance with us!"

She shakes her head. "We should get going. I'll be out on the deck."

She picks up her salad and pushes through the screen door. I look at Paige and she shrugs at me.

"Maybe she doesn't like music," she says.

It's starting to become obvious that Talia and I aren't cut out to be friends. I feel like I've done my best, and she hasn't made any effort at all. Maybe it was too much to ask for the two of us to become close, considering our parents are barely on speaking terms.

At least Paige is oblivious to any tension. As we make our way around the lake toward the barbecue, she chatters incessantly about her mystery, like Nancy Drew after a couple of espressos.

"I wonder if there was some kind of dramatic falling out," she says. "Like maybe Frank was a spy, and they found out, and Mom ratted him out to the authorities, and Uncle Gary was upset because Frank had started to turn him to the dark side."

I laugh. "You think so? What would a spy be doing in cottage country?"

She shrugs. "The government probably has secret spy detachments all over the place."

"Maybe there's a satellite tracking bunker hidden underneath the ice cream shop," I say.

"That's quite possible," says Paige.

"You realize Frank probably has nothing to do with Mom and Gary not talking," says Talia, the perpetual wet blanket. "Families get estranged all the time, for all kinds of reasons. Anyway, I don't think Gary and your mom ever got along that well."

I think Talia is probably right, but it annoys me that she can't go along with Paige for just five minutes. "Maybe he was an alien, Paige," I say. "Maybe he landed here with an important message, but he and Mom fell in love, and when Gary learned of their plan to take off for Frank's home planet, he told Grandpa and Grandma and thwarted it, keeping Mom from her one true love."

"Mom really shouldn't be angry about that anymore," says Paige. "If she'd taken off into space, you and I wouldn't be here."

"That's true," I say. "We owe Uncle Gary a big fat thank you."

"You guys watch too much TV," says Talia. She hugs the bowl of salad tightly to her chest, then steps up from the beach onto Mariana's lawn.

Mr. Foer is standing on the deck, drinking a beer and standing over a grill. He waves as we approach.

"Come on up!" he calls.

As we climb the steps to the cottage, Rosie galumphs across the deck toward us and comes to a rolling stop by our feet. Paige immediately drops to the floor and begins to play with the puppy as Mariana appears in the door to greet us.

"Smells good," I say.

"Dad's cooking rib eyes," says Mariana. She eyes Talia's salad. "That looks amazing. What is it?"

"It's a Greek pasta salad," says Talia. "I just kind of tossed everything in the fridge into it."

"Yum," says Mariana, taking the salad and carrying it to the picnic table. "You guys want a drink?"

"Nonalcoholic," her father says. "I'm sorry kids, but I'm not one of those cool dads you hear about."

"Don't be silly," says Mariana, leaning in to give her father a quick hug from the side. "Nobody would ever confuse you for a cool dad. Is soda all right with you guys?"

Paige nods enthusiastically. We aren't allowed much soda at home.

"I'll help you," says Talia, following Mariana into the cottage.

Mr. Foer flips the steaks, futzes with the heat, and closes the lid, then turns to give us his full attention. "So, you guys are the Tremblay grandkids."

"Yes," I say. "Our mother is Janet, and Gary is Talia's dad."

He takes a sip of his beer, nodding slowly. "I can see the resemblance. I haven't seen your parents in many, many years."

Paige gives me an excited look, then turns back to Mr. Foer. "Did you know them when you were a teenager?" she asks.

He smiles and nods. "I did. There were a lot of young people around our age back then. We had a lot of fun, to say the least."

"Did you know a guy named Frank?" she asks eagerly.

A funny look flickers across his face, and he gives Paige a sideways grin. "Frank? As a matter of fact, I knew him really well. Still do."

"You do?" asks Paige, leaning forward, her eyes wide. "Do you know where he is now?"

"Well, right now he's sitting on a deck having a chat with a nice young woman," he says with a laugh.

Paige's eyes open wide. "You're Frank?" she asks as Mariana and Talia return with tall glasses of iced soda. "Talia! Guess what? Mr. Foer is Frank!"

"Really?" Talia glances at me, and I nod to confirm.

"What are you talking about?" asks Mariana.

"Your dad used to hang out with our mom and Uncle Gary," I explain.

"He was the honorary Tremblay," says Paige. "We found a photo album of the three of them."

"Crazy!" says Mariana. "What a coincidence."

"Small world," Mr. Foer—Frank—agrees. "We were really close, it's true, but then my folks sold our cottage and I didn't come back the next year. It was harder to keep up back then. There was no Facebook or social media, and we were all starting out on our lives. Haven't heard from either of your parents since. Anyway," he says as he lifts steaks off the grill onto a large platter. "Have a seat. Dinner is served."

I can tell by the way Paige slumps into her seat that she's disappointed in this straightforward explanation. She was obviously hoping for something more dramatic.

"I always wanted to bring Mariana to the lake," says her father. "She'll be graduating at the end of the year, and I figured that if I didn't do it now, it would never happen."

"What he really means," says Mariana, "is that he wanted to take a trip down memory lane, and he insisted that I come along. We've been here since the day school got out."

"You're not all that disappointed, are you?" he asks her as he pulls up a chair at the end of the table.

"No," she says. "I'm just teasing you. It's been just as good as you promised. Cute boys everywhere." She gives me an exaggerated wink. Her father lifts a skeptical eyebrow.

"Don't worry, Mr. Foer," I say, raising my hands, palms out. "Mariana is barking up the wrong tree if she's referring to me."

"Mark's gay," says Paige matter-of-factly as she scoops some of Talia's salad onto a plate.

"Paige," says Talia, "remember what I said about outing people?"

"Yes," says Paige, "and I've thought about it. I don't like that rule. It's totally fine that Mark is gay, and if it bugs anyone, that's their problem."

"Yes," says Talia, "but that's not really the point. I think—"

I cut her off. I don't have the energy for one of her political debates. "It's fine, Talia. I don't care if she outs me."

"You're pretty privileged to feel that way," she says.

"Fine," I say. "I'm privileged."

She looks like she wants to say something else but thinks better of it and instead stares down at her plate and begins furiously attacking her salad.

"Talia," says Mr. Foer. "Tell me about what your father's been up to. Do you guys live in Toronto?"

"No," she says. "We live in Victoria. He moved to BC after college and took a job with the province. That's where he met my mother."

"Is she here with you, too?" he asks.

Talia shakes her head. "No, they split up when I was little. She lives up island."

"Well, it's good that you can be close to both of them," he says. Talia nods, noncommittally. I realize that I don't really know much about the situation with her mother. I wonder how she'd react if I asked.

After dinner, I help Mariana clear the table. Talia was right about the cottage; inside it's much nicer than ours. It's obviously been renovated in the past few years. The furniture matches, and the kitchen is rustic but it's deliberate, like it was planned by an interior designer.

"Nice digs," I say as we load the dishwasher.

She shrugs. "It's nice. Not cozy like yours, though. This place has no soul."

I rinse plates and hand them to her.

"Talia mentioned that you've been spending time with Darren," she says as she's bending.

"Yeah," I say. "He's been helping me with my grandfather's old Mustang."

"Hmmm," she says.

"That sounds like the kind of noise that's filling in for something," I say.

She shuts the dishwasher and looks at me, smiling. "I don't know Darren all that well," she says. "But I've heard stories, and I know enough to tell you to watch out."

"Watch out for what?" I ask her.

"Just don't let him give you the wrong idea, that's all I mean. I'm not sure Darren is exactly what he seems to be."

"I'll be fine," I say. "I don't mind a bit of mystery in a guy."

"Mystery isn't really what I'm getting at," she says. "But suit yourself. Just don't say I didn't warn you."

CHAPTER TWELVE

TALIA

Paige is kind of an amazing kid, I think, as she skips ahead of me down the road back from having an ice-cream lunch in the village. I'd never thought much about having cousins—and my mom's an only child, so Mark and Paige are the only ones I have—but there's something cool about it. I mean, Paige will always be my cousin. It's not like a friendship, where no matter how close you are, you could eventually drift apart. Anyway, I'm glad I've had a chance to get to know her. Not glad we're stuck in the woods or anything—but Paige is the silver lining in this situation I guess.

Though, if Paige is a silver lining, Mark's the cloud that's making this week suck. Or maybe, to be fair, Erin's the actual storm cloud, the big, dark, towering cumulonimbus or whatever they're called. Erin's the one who's made me feel like this: achy and hollow and irritable and kind of stupidly hopeless, like I'll never feel truly happy again.

Mark's just a lazy little rain cloud drizzling all over my already bad mood.

"Cheer up," Paige says, turning and waiting for me to catch up. She's licked her ice cream cone to a sharp point and is catching the drips with her tongue. "Mark says he'll come canoeing with us this afternoon."

Gotta love how he was too busy to help with the packing all morning but suddenly has time to play on the lake. But Paige looks excited, and I can't bring myself to disappoint her. "Awesome," I say, forcing a grin. "That'll be fun."

———

Back at the cottage, Paige and I make sandwiches for lunch. "You know," I say, slicing tomatoes, "I was thinking about last night? At the barbecue? I get that Mark doesn't care who knows he's gay. And it's cool that it's not a big deal to you. But you should keep in mind that not everyone is like that. I mean, some people really wouldn't want you outing them."

"Like you?"

I hesitate. "I'm out to everyone at school and in my family and stuff, so it's not like it's a secret. But I guess I think it should be up to me who I tell."

"I don't see why it should be different," Paige says.

"Different from what?"

"Like, different from straight people. Everyone outs them all the time. Like, I'd just say, 'Oh, this is my cousin and her boyfriend.' I mean, if you had a boyfriend. So that'd be telling everyone you were straight."

"Or bi. Or pan."

"Yeah. Okay, or bi or pan. But if I say, 'This is my cousin and her . . . her nonbinary partner . . .'"

I shake my head. "Then you'd have outed Erin as nonbinary. And transphobia is a real thing, and it's dangerous. And anyway, it isn't yours to share."

"If it were me, I wouldn't want people treating me differently from everyone else."

"Well, it isn't you."

Paige shoots me a sideways look. "You don't know that."

She's right: I just made a big assumption, the kind of assumption that I'm always annoyed at other people for making. "Sorry," I say. "Uh. Are you . . ."

She shrugs. "How would I know? I'm a kid."

"Some kids know," I say. "But yeah, I didn't either."

"Mark says he knew when he was, like, six." Paige wrinkles her nose. "But he might just be saying that."

"Who's saying what?" Mark says, banging in through the doorway and dumping an armload of dirty rags on the floor. "Oh—you've made lunch? Awesome."

I roll my eyes. "Nice timing."

"We're going to take a picnic," Paige says. "In the canoe."

Mark leans over the counter, picks up a piece of tomato and pops it in his mouth. "So I guess that's it for your investigation. Huh, Nancy Drew?"

Paige shrugs. "I guess so. Do you really think Mom and Uncle Gary just decided to stop being brother and sister?"

"I don't think it's like that exactly, Paige," I say. "Some people just don't get along."

"In a way, it's good, right?" Mark asks her. "I mean, if they're just going to bicker and argue, why bother getting together in the first place?"

Paige looks at us like we've grown third eyeballs. "I think it's stupid. We could have been coming here every summer, but the fun's all spoiled because they're both so stubborn. Isn't that what grown-ups are always telling kids? Try to resolve your differences? When you and I argue, Mom is always telling us to meet halfway. Why can't she and Gary do that?"

I grin at Mark. "Hard to disagree. You are one smart kid, Paige."

She rolls her eyes. "Yeah, well, anyway, you guys promised you'd come out in the canoe."

Mark shrugs. "Why not? Darren's got stuff to do this afternoon anyway."

Paige gets a sly look on her face. "You like him, don't you? I mean, you LIKE him."

He ignores her and reaches for another tomato slice. I shove his hand away. "Cut it out, or there'll be none for the sandwiches. Grab the cheese from the fridge, would you?"

Mark passes me a block of cheddar. "You know who doesn't like Darren?" I say. "Mariana. She is not a fan."

"Yeah, I got that last night," he says. "You think they went out or something?"

"Didn't get that impression. She just said he can be kind of an asshole. Maybe you should, I don't know, be careful?"

"Yeah, thanks for that, Talia. When I want relationship advice from you, I'll let you know."

"Fine, whatever." I start slapping sandwiches together: bread, mayo, tomato, lettuce, cheese. Relationship advice. What a jerk.

Out on the lake, I feel happier. More peaceful. It is beautiful: the sky a soft clear blue, the sun warm on my face and bare arms. The water is glassy smooth and the trees along the shoreline are reflected in it so clearly that they look as if they are growing both up and down. Even the air smells good.

And there's no cell service, which means for once I am not waiting hopefully for the vibration of my phone in my pocket. Not waiting for Erin's latest message to determine my mood for the day. It's a relief. Which makes me wonder if actually, finally, definitely breaking up would be better than this painful uncertainty.

"Look!" Paige shouts, pointing.

I follow her gaze and see a ripple in the water.

"A fish! It jumped right out of the lake!"

"Should've brought fishing gear," Mark says. "Could catch ourselves some bass for dinner."

"That's mean," Paige says, and my eyes meet Mark's.

"RIP fish," he says.

I laugh.

"What?" Paige demands, sensing a joke she's left out of.

"We must've been about the age she is now," Mark says, nodding at Paige. "Crazy, huh?"

"WHAT IS?" Paige shifts on her seat, wobbling the canoe.

"When we were here before," I tell her, "when Mark and I were about your age, maybe a little older, we caught a fish. Just stuck a line in the water, kind of playing at fishing, and then—"

"We got a bite! And I pulled it in . . ."

"This big," I say, holding my hands about eight inches apart.

"I wanted to cook it for dinner," Mark says, "but Talia—"

"I wanted to set it free," I say, remembering the shocking unexpectedness of it: the panicked flopping of the fish, the slipperiness of it, the brutal hook hopelessly twisted into the roof of its mouth. The horrible realization that we had done this to it. "But it died."

Paige looks like she might cry.

"So we had a funeral," Mark says. "Talia even said a little prayer."

"Did I?" I've been an atheist for as long as I can remember.

"Yeah, totally. 'Dear God, please take care of this fish. He was a good fish.'" Mark winks at me. "Or something like that."

"That's so sad," Paige says.

"It was," I say. But I can't help smiling at this little piece of my childhood.

"I'm glad we're here, you know?" Mark says. "I mean, not about Grandma and everything. Obviously. But—"

"Yeah," I say. "I know. Me too."

———

We paddle out into the middle of the lake, and then float around for a while, chatting and joking, and Paige makes us sing "Row, Row, Row Your Boat" as a round, which is pretty hilarious. Paige can really sing. Her voice is lovely, but Mark and I are hopeless. I'm practically tone-deaf, and he keeps starting at the wrong time and messing us all up. We eat our sandwiches and eventually make our way back to the dock. Mark convinces Paige and me to jump in and swim the last few hundred yards back while he paddles alongside. Paige zips ahead, showing off an impressively professional front crawl. I flip onto my back and stare up at the sky for a few minutes, watching the few tiny white clouds moving ever so slowly. My ears are underwater and everything is silent and peaceful. I shut my eyes and feel the sun warm on my face, bright even behind my closed eyelids.

"Hurry up, slow poke!" Paige yells. She's standing on the dock, waiting for me while Mark unloads our stuff from the canoe. I wave at her and start swimming.

We forgot to pack towels, so Paige and I have to put our T-shirts and shorts back on over our wet swimsuits. Mark slings our now-empty picnic bag over his shoulder, and we head off up the trail through the trees. I love how quiet it is here.

"Hey, you guys want to see something cool?" Mark says.

"Sure!" Paige bounces along at his side.

"Grandpa's car! Darren and I got the engine running yesterday. It's pretty awesome."

Paige wrinkles her nose. "Having an engine that works isn't that cool, Mark. All cars have that."

"Yeah, but this one . . ." He shoves her. "Are you messing with me?"

She giggles. "Yeah. Okay, sure, you can show us. Right, Talia?"

Mark turns to look at me, and I can suddenly see the resemblance between the two of them. Same eyes, same wide smile and one-sided dimple, same neat square chin. And they're both looking at me with the same eager, uncomplicated, hopeful expression.

"Sure," I say, because how could I say anything else. "Show us your car."

CHAPTER THIRTEEN

MARK

As we wind up the path toward the cottage, I'm cautiously optimistic that Talia is starting to warm up to me. I almost make a comment to that effect, but I manage to bite my tongue. Probably not a great idea to push my luck just yet.

I am, however, formulating a plan to keep a good thing going. First, I'll show off the car, then I'll convince Talia that we should all go for a quick joyride around the lake. We'll stop for ice cream and show off how cool we are. Finally, I'll offer to teach her how to drive. If that doesn't melt away the last of her facade, I don't know what will. In any case, I'm banking on it, since I intend to take advantage of her goodwill and ask her to watch Paige while Darren and I head into town for the evening.

I'm not sure I'd call it a date. More like loose plans to hang out in glamorous downtown Bracebridge. But it was his idea, and I'm choosing to take it as a good sign that he wants to hang out with me alone. If he's got even a tiny bit of interest in me, I'm determined to tease it out of him.

As we move toward the shed, I glance behind me and see the shine of a good day reflected in each of their faces. Paige is beaming, and Talia is more relaxed than I've seen her looking since we arrived at the lake. She catches me looking at her and her eyes drop. As if trying to prove that she's not really in such a good mood, she reaches into her pocket and pulls out her phone.

"Nuh-uh," I say. "Not yet. I don't want you guys distracted from my big reveal."

"I've already seen the car, Mark," Talia says.

"I know, but you haven't seen it *working*. Just five minutes, okay?"

She rolls her eyes but puts her phone away as we reach the shed.

The door to the shed is slightly open, which surprises me, since I'm almost sure I locked it when Darren and I finished up yesterday. But I shrug it off. Must have forgotten.

"Okay," I say. "Close your eyes and count to ten!"

"Mark," says Talia, "quit fooling around."

"Okay, fine," I say. "Come on in."

There's a loud clatter from the back of the shed as I push open the door. It takes a second for my eyes to adjust to the dark, then I see a figure at the back of the shed, near the workbench. It's Darren.

"Hey!" he says in a cheerful rush. "You're back!"

"What's going on?" I ask as I walk into the dimness of the shed, Talia and Paige close behind.

"I stopped by to see if you were around," he says. "Thought we could work on the car for a while. I didn't find you in here, so I figured I'd tweak around under the hood a bit. You don't mind, do you?"

"Uh, no," I say. "I guess not." It's kind of weird that he just walked in, but since he came all this way, I guess it kind of makes sense.

"What was that crash?" asks Talia.

"Oh, yeah," says Darren with an awkward laugh. "It was really hot in here, so I opened the window. Knocked a couple of paint cans off the shelf when I was leaning across the workbench."

"I was just going to show Talia and Paige the Mustang," I say.

"Oh, yeah," he says. "Cool. You guys should get in, start it up. It's a sweet ride." He looks past me and his expression shifts, and when Talia and I turn around to see what he's looking at, Paige is gone. She's probably bored with all the car talk.

"Come on," I say to Talia, opening the driver's-side door. "You want to get behind the wheel and turn her over?"

She shakes her head. "I don't drive, thanks."

"I could teach you," I say. "It'd be fun!"

She looks skeptical. "I'm not sure about that."

"I should probably get going," says Darren. "I just remembered that I'm supposed to be helping my uncle with something."

Talia looks back and forth between us, as if she's trying to figure something out.

"Mark!" I hear Paige yell from outside. "Talia! Come here!"

We follow the sound of her voice outside and around to the side of the shed where it butts up against the woods. She's kneeling underneath the window.

"What's going on?" I ask, but before she has the chance to answer, I notice the pile of tools on the ground underneath the open window.

"Wow," says Talia.

I feel my neck getting hot as I put two and two together.

"Where is he?" I ask. I don't wait for an answer, hurrying back around to the shed door and sticking my head inside just long enough to confirm that Darren's already gone.

I head up the driveway, breaking into a run as I catch sight of his back through the trees. I overtake him as he's about to reach his car, a souped-up sedan that's parked up on the edge of the road, just out of sight of the cottage.

"What's the big idea?" I yell at his back as I approach him. He freezes, and, for a second, I think he's going to run for his car, but instead he turns around and shrugs, giving me a glimpse of an unpleasant smile that I've never seen before.

"You win some, you lose some," he says.

"Win some?" I ask. "I think you mean steal some."

"A bunch of old tools, man. Tools that would probably get tossed anyway, once your folks sell this place." I can tell by the breezy way he says it that he actually believes he hasn't done anything wrong. What's worse, the smirk on his face tells me I've been fooling myself to think he was interested in me. Was he pretending to flirt with me so he could pull this scam? Or was I just so caught up in the idea of hooking up with the hot bad boy that I let myself imagine something that wasn't even there?

Either way, I feel like a complete idiot.

"You really are a dirtbag, aren't you?" I ask.

He laughs and throws his hands in the air. "You caught me, dude. Now why don't you cut the drama queen act and move on with your life instead of acting like a little bitch?"

He turns back toward his car, but before I even know what's happening I'm across the road, shoving my hand against the car door before he can open it.

"Get the fuck out of my way," he says.

Instead, I move closer to him. I'm not a fighter, but I am a good couple of inches taller than Darren, and pretty fit, and I'm surprised at the sense of satisfaction I feel when he defensively steps back from me. Then, for a split second, I imagine Talia telling me that I'm acting like a typical testosterone-driven male, trying to solve problems with force. I back up, crossing my arms in front of my chest.

"I thought you were helping me because we were friends," I say. "Not so you could dig around and help yourself to someone else's property."

He smirks. "You're trying to tell me you didn't have ulterior motives of your own?"

I feel myself flush. "I don't know what you're talking about."

"Oh, sure you do," he says. "You've been flirting with me since I first helped walk you back from Mariana's place." He flutters his eyelids at me, and then tilts his head in an exaggeratedly coquettish pose. "Thorry, thweetheart," he says, faking a lisp. "I'm not into boyth."

I've never really understood what it means to "see red," but now I think I understand. I feel an involuntary twitch in my legs, and I'm about to lunge at him when someone screams.

"Mark!" We both turn to look across the road, to where Paige is standing at the top of the drive, Talia walking up behind her. "Don't be an idiot!"

"Yeah, Mark," says Darren, pushing past me and yanking his car door open. "Don't do anything you'll end up regretting."

He gets into his car and disappears down the road in a cloud of dust.

"This is crazy!" says Paige. "We need to call the police! We need to call someone at the newspaper!"

"Take it easy, Paige," I say.

"What do you mean, 'take it easy'?" she says. "We were almost robbed!"

"It was a bunch of stupid old tools, Paige, okay?" I snap. I turn away from her hurt expression and start back toward the cottage.

"Are you okay?" Talia asks, jogging to keep step with me. "Did he say something?"

"Yes, Talia," I say. "You were right, of course. Turns out he's an asshole just like you and Mariana warned me about. He's also a homophobe, which I'm sure is extra exciting for you."

"What the hell is that supposed to mean?" she asks.

"Oh, I don't know," I say, stopping at the deck and turning to look at her. "Just that you don't seem happy unless you have some social justice warrior shit to keep you busy."

She opens her mouth to respond, but I don't feel like listening to another lecture, so I turn to go inside. On my way, I push the screen door open as far as it will go, finding some small satisfaction when it slams shut behind me.

I spend the rest of the afternoon curled up on the tiny bed in my room, flipping absentmindedly through some of the ancient comics I found in a box under the bed. I try to forget about the episode with Darren, but it's hard. I've never had anyone speak to me that way. The fact that it was somebody I thought I was becoming friends with—if I'm being honest, thought I might have a chance with—only makes it worse.

My phone rings and I yank it from my pocket, stupidly wondering for a split second if it's Darren calling to apologize. It's just Jareth, though. I consider answering, telling him that it's time to consider breaking up, but I don't have it in me. I wish he would finally get the hint.

At some point, I hear Paige and Talia come inside and start moving quietly about the kitchen, preparing something to eat. Part of me wants to go out and offer to help, to somehow bring things back to the way they were on the lake, but I doubt they want to hang out with me after I was such a dick. Eventually, I hear the screen door open and close again, and footsteps on the deck tell me they've taken their supper outside to eat.

This isn't how I pictured this trip playing out. The Pride Parade is the day after tomorrow, and after the day I've had, I wish more than anything that I could just leave this stupid cottage and spend the weekend partying in Toronto.

I sit up with a burst of inspiration. Why *can't* I leave this stupid cottage? I'm not contributing much, as Talia is so fond of pointing out, and she and Paige are having a fine time hanging out without me. Most important, however, there's a car just sitting in the shed, waiting for someone to take advantage of it. I allow myself to imagine pulling up to the side of the street in Toronto in a sexy vintage sports car, a pride flag draped across the hood.

To hell with Darren. There are a million cute guys in Toronto just dying to hang out with someone like me. Life is an adventure, right?

I pack my duffel in about five minutes flat. Moving quietly through the cottage, careful not to let the screen door slam, I slide out of the cottage and then run across the backyard to the shed.

The Mustang is louder than I'd hoped, but at least it starts on the first try. I rub my hands on the steering wheel for a moment, excited that my plan has fallen into place this easily, then I throw her into reverse and slowly back out of the shed.

CHAPTER FOURTEEN

TALIA

"What was that?" Paige says.

"That loud noise that sounded like a lion coughing up a hairball?" I roll my eyes. "That'd be Mark playing with his precious—"

"But where's he going?" Paige asks, pointing.

I put down my fork. Grandpa's car is reversing out of the shed and down the driveway. Mark's probably just taking it for a test drive—almost certainly that's all he's doing—but I suddenly get this bad feeling. He was pretty upset about Darren—I think he had a real crush on him—and I don't know what he's planning to do, but I don't think we should just let him go. "Paige? Do you think . . ." And I'm running down the driveway with Paige at my heels.

I reach the end of the driveway at the same time he does, and I bang both my hands against his window. "Mark, wait!"

He looks pissed off, but he stops and rolls down the window. "What now?"

"Where are you going?"

"Nowhere. Just a drive, all right?"

Paige sticks her head in the open window. "Why do you have your duffel bag, then? Are you running away?"

My eyes fall on the stuffed duffel sitting on the back seat. "Mark?"

He groans, bangs his head back against the seat, and shuts off the engine. "Fine. Yes. I'm out of here."

"Uh, no. I don't think so," I say.

"Just for a couple of days," he says. "I need to get away, all right? That asshole Darren . . ."

I nod. "I know. It sucks. But—"

"And it's Pride weekend," he says. "I've always wanted to go to Toronto Pride. And we're so close . . ."

Toronto Pride. My heart does a weird extra beat. "You're . . . you're going to Toronto?"

"Was going to," he says. "But I suppose you'd be straight on the phone with my mom, complaining that I abandoned you and Paige and my all my cottage-related responsibilities . . ."

Toronto. Erin. Toronto Pride. It's all less than a three-hour drive away. And we have a car. I can't believe I'm even considering this, but the words are out of my mouth before I can change my mind. "Not if you take me with you," I say.

Paige straightens up and plants her hands on her hips. "Hello? Hello? You guys can't leave me here. I'm ten years old, remember?"

Mark is looking back and forth from me to Paige and then back to me. His forehead creases and I can practically see his dreams dying, clear as little rainbow-tinted thought bubbles bursting above his head. Gay bars, nightclubs, up all night dancing with cute guys? Nope, he'll be hanging out with his sister at the rainbow bouncy castle.

"Of course we can't," I say. "You're coming, too, Paige. Let's go pack our bags." I hold out my hand to Mark. "Keys, please."

He looks wounded. "You think I'd take off? You don't trust me to wait?"

I just stand there, hand out.

He turns off the ignition and drops the keys in my palm. He looks like a kicked puppy, but I push my guilt aside. I'm still pissed about the "social justice warrior" shit he said earlier. As if caring about social justice is a bad thing. It actually makes my heart race just thinking about it—but I guess we'll have plenty of time to talk about that on our way to Toronto.

Oh my god. We're going to Toronto. WE ARE GOING TO TORONTO.

———

Twenty minutes later, we're packed up and on the road. Paige is bouncing around in the back seat talking nonstop about how she can't believe we are doing this and how her mom is going to be so mad. Mark is ignoring her, eyes on the road and hands on the wheel. And I'm texting Erin.

Guess what? Coming down to the city for Pride weekend.

Erin's reply is instant. Talia!!! That is so fantastic.

Be there in about three hours. By nine o'clock. I almost attach a heart emoji but change my mind. It's weird to feel so uncertain with the one person that knows me better than anyone else in the world. Did we for sure break up, or not quite? Are we getting back together? Or are we just staying friends? I honestly don't know. Can't wait to see you, I type.

I'm working until midnight. Can you come to the Village? Come to the cafe?

I suddenly realize Mark and I haven't even talked about where we're going to go. Or where we're going to sleep tonight. I glance in the mirror at Paige and feel a flood of guilt. I'm taking a ten-year-old to Toronto with absolutely no plan for how to take care of her.

"Mark?" I want to talk to him without Paige listening, but there's no way to do that. "Uh, can we stop for a bathroom break at the next gas station?"

"Already? Seriously? We just left."

I try to communicate with my eyes, but he refuses to look my way. Like he's mad at me. Which is ridiculous, because he's the one who's been a total jerk.

Well, whatever. Paige is his sister. He'll just have to deal.

Absolutely, I type. Will see you SOON.

Maybe ten minutes later, I spot a Tim Horton's and elbow Mark. "Pull over. I want a coffee and a pee."

He rolls his eyes but turns left into the parking lot. Paige and I head inside, and he waits in the car. We get in line behind three elderly men who are arguing about what kind of donuts should make up their dozen: *Kathleen likes those Boston Cream ones! No, no, the best are the Walnut Crunch...*

I turn to Paige. "Hold our spot in line—I forgot my wallet." And I dash back out to the car and knock on Mark's window.

"Jesus, you startled me. What?"

"We have to talk. What exactly are you planning to do with your sister? I'm meeting up with Erin. You can't take her to a nightclub, you know. And you can't just leave her in the car, parked somewhere, while you go party."

"Jesus, Talia. Give me some credit, okay? I'm actually not as much of an asshole as you apparently think I am."

"Sorry." I glance back over my shoulder at the donut shop. "I didn't want to talk about it in front of her."

"I thought I'd drop her at the hospital," he says. "With Mom."

"Seriously? Then they'll know we're in the city. They'll freak out."

"Sure, but what can they do about it? We'll already be there."

I shake my head. "Dad'll order us to turn right around and drive straight back to the cottage."

"You're eighteen, Talia. He can't really tell you what to do."

I blow out an exasperated breath. Dad and I have a really good relationship. He almost never tells me what to do, but I almost never break the unspoken rules either.

The door to the Timmy's opens and Paige sticks her head out. "Uh, guys? I don't have any money . . ."

"Coming!" I yell. Then I bend back down to Mark. "Figure it out," I tell him. "Because I have plans, and they don't include babysitting for you."

———————

By the time we've eaten our box of Timbits and I'm down to the last cold dregs of milky coffee, we've just passed Orillia and the highway signs are counting down the distance to Barrie. I'm mentally rehashing the last in-person conversation I had with Erin, where we talked about open relationships. Why does it feel so . . . uncool . . . to want to be monogamous? I totally get all the arguments for being poly, and it's not like I think there's anything wrong with it. I mean, if it works for you, that's great. I just know it wouldn't work for me. I hate the thought of Erin being with other people. And I have no interest in being with anyone else. The truth is, the category of people I'm attracted to is like the middle of some weird Venn diagram—it's a tiny little intersection with just Erin in it.

Though Erin says I just need to get out more.

My phone buzzes. And at that same moment, the car makes an awful noise. Not the lion-coughing-up-a-hairball noise. This is more of a ghastly metallic *clunk*.

"What was that?" Paige asks.

"Shit, shit, shit!" Mark yells.

"Pull over," I say. "Pull over."

"Where?" he asks, slowing the car to a crawl. "There's nowhere to . . . Look at the map, Talia. Where's the next exit?"

A truck passes us, leaning on the horn as it flies by. I open the Google Maps app, but there's just a blue dot in the middle of an empty grid. "Shit," I say. "There's no service."

"Uh oh," Paige says, and her voice is a little too high-pitched. "Is the car on fire?"

I look up from my phone. Black smoke is billowing from under the hood.

"Shit, shit, shit!" Mark yells again. "Talia—"

Then I spot something up ahead. "There's a turnoff—look, coming up—"

"What if the car explodes!" Paige cries out. "Gas is flammable, you know. I think we should stop. We should get out. We should—"

"Shut UP, Paige!" Mark yells, and he spins the wheel to the right, taking the exit.

He drives a few hundred yards, past what looks like a diner, and pulls over onto the gravel at the side of the road. Paige leaps out of the car before it's even come to a complete stop, and we both follow, Mark killing the engine and popping the hood on his way.

Then we all stand there, staring. There's a massive plume of stinky black smoke pouring from the car. And it looks like we're in the middle of fucking nowhere.

CHAPTER FIFTEEN

MARK

This isn't how I pictured things playing out. I was supposed to arrive in Toronto alone, music blasting from the open windows, turning heads and breaking hearts before I'd even pulled up to the curb and stepped out of the car.

Instead, the three of us are standing on the side of the road, just off the highway, listening to the well-functioning automobiles up above zooming merrily along to their destinations.

A few feet away, Grandpa's car sits and stares reproachfully into the distance, the waft of black smoke from beneath the hood gradually dissipating until it's just a wisp, then gone altogether. There's a pause, and then a distinct *pop* from beneath the hood, followed by a long, drawn-out whistle that comes to a sad, sputtering finish.

"Well, this is fun," says Paige.

I move toward the car.

"Stop!" yells Talia. "We don't know if it's safe."

"I'm pretty sure it is," I say. "It's stopped smoking."

As I approach the Mustang, I get the distinct impression that it's dead, that our joyride has killed it. I climb in behind the wheel and after a moment of hesitation, I turn the key. Nothing happens.

"Shit," I mutter. I grab the keys and get back out of the car.

Talia and Paige haven't moved. They're keeping a safe distance, standing close to one another on the other side of the road.

"It's not going to explode," I call across. "It's not going to do much of anything, as far as I can tell."

They exchange a glance, then walk over to join me.

"What do we do now?" asks Paige.

I look at Talia. "Do you have service?"

She shakes her head, and I pull my own phone out of my pocket. No bars.

"Goddammit," I say. I look up and down the road in both directions. There's not a sign of anything, except for the diner back in the shadow of the off-ramp. "Well, Paige, looks like today is your lucky day. Time for a milkshake."

We get our stuff out of the car and lock it, although it's clear that nobody is going to be driving it anywhere without a lot of work.

The diner looks like it hasn't changed since the fifties. Long and low, white with baby blue accent panels and a large neon sign that reads *Shirley's*. The bell on the front door jingles to announce our arrival as we step inside, and for a moment, I wonder if the place is open at all. It's totally empty, the cash register unmanned, and the booths sit vacant in the dim slatted light cast by the half-drawn venetian blinds.

It smells like fresh coffee, though, and as we stand there in the doorway wondering what to do, someone yells from the back.

"Grab a seat wherever you like! I'll be with you in a moment!"

We grab a booth at the back of the restaurant, nestled into the corner with a distant view of the Mustang sitting forlorn by the side of the road.

"This is really cool," says Paige, twisting in her seat to look around the restaurant. "It's like we stepped into a time machine."

There's some clattering, then a dramatic crash from the kitchen, and a moment later a woman comes out from the swinging chrome door. She looks to be around sixty, or maybe a bit older, and she's wearing a jumpsuit, the same baby blue color as the outside of the diner, with an apron tied over the top of it. Her hair, a mass of blond curls, is pulled into a dramatic high ponytail, tied slightly to the side with a large pink bow.

"Hello!" she says as her high heels *clickety-clack* across the diner toward us. She has a coffeepot in one hand, some menus

130

in the other. "Strangers! I love strangers." She stops at our booth and drops the menus in front of us. "Coffee?"

Talia and I nod, and she reaches over to pour for us. "How about you, sweetie?" she asks Paige.

"I'll have a strawberry milkshake, please," says Paige. "Are you Shirley?"

The lady laughs. "Sort of. The Shirley on the sign was my mother, rest her soul. I'm Shirley Jr."

"Do you have Wi-Fi?" asks Talia, a slightly frantic tone to her voice.

"Nope. Sorry, hon," says Shirley Jr.

Next to me in the booth, Talia looks as deflated as a week-old birthday balloon. She takes one last, sad look at her phone, then tucks it back into her pocket.

"You guys take a minute with the menus," says Shirley Jr. "I'll be back with your shake."

She clacks back to the kitchen.

"I'm starving," I say, beginning to scan the menu.

"Are you worried at all?" asks Talia. "We're stuck in the middle of nowhere, and the car's broken down. Don't you realize how much trouble we're going to be in?"

"Well, if that's the case, I don't see the point of being hungry, too," I say. "Let's eat something and then regroup."

A loud, somewhat erratic whirring sound comes from the kitchen, followed by another series of crashes and bangs.

"Maybe she'll let us use the phone," says Paige.

"I'm sure she will," I say. "We'll figure it out."

Talia looks at me with something like amazement. "Does anything stress you out?" she asks. "Don't you have any sense of self-preservation?"

"I guess I just don't see the point of constantly worrying," I say. "We're on an adventure!"

"It is kind of exciting," says Paige. I can tell from the look on Talia's face that she doesn't agree, but she doesn't bother to argue. She just pulls her phone out again and stares at it longingly.

"Maybe if you close your eyes and wish hard enough, it will magically start to work," I say.

"I have plans to meet Erin," she says. "If I don't get in touch, they might be worried, or pissed off."

"They won't be mad," I say. "It's totally out of your control. Just think of the story you'll be able to tell."

The kitchen door swings open again, and Shirley Jr. approaches with a tray. She places a tall frilly glass, pink with milkshake, in front of Paige, followed by the metal mixing cup, also half full of milkshake.

"That's so you don't run out too quick," she says with a wink. "So, what brings you kids into this place?"

"Our car broke down," says Talia. She points out the window, and Shirley Jr. stretches past us to glance down the road.

"Well, that's a pain in the patoot," she says.

"Is there a service station around here?" I ask.

"There is," she says. "About half a kilometer down the road."

All three of us perk up with expectation.

"Only problem is, it's been closed for about ten years," says Shirley. "Now, what can I get for you?"

———

As we wait for our food, I try to think about some options.

"This is my fault," I say finally. "I never should have trusted the Mustang to get us to Toronto. After lunch, I'm going to hitchhike to the next major exit and try to find help."

"You can't hitchhike," says Paige. "It's dangerous and stupid."

"She's right," says Talia. "We'll have to figure something else out."

The door swings open again, and Shirley Jr. approaches with a tray piled high with food.

"Would I be able to use your phone?" I ask her. "We're really stuck, and I need to figure out how to get the car fixed."

"You're welcome to the phone, honey," she says. "But you might want to wait until Babs gets here."

"Babs?" I ask, confused.

"Yeah," she says as she leans across me to drop a plate of fries in front of Talia. "My wife, Babs. She's a retired mechanic.

I just called her. She's going to get her tools together and head on over."

———

After lunch we stroll back to the Mustang. Shirley Jr. joins us, sitting on the trunk and keeping one eye on the diner in case any customers show up.

"It's unlikely," she explains. "We're not really on anyone's radar, ever since the giant truck stop opened up down the highway a few years back. To tell you the truth, I'm probably going to close up shop for good at the end of the summer."

"That's sad," says Paige.

"Yeah," says Shirley Jr. "Shirley Sr. opened this place when I was just a kid, and when she died Babs and I moved home to take it over. But it's like my mom used to say: 'When a door closes, a window opens.' Babs and I are probably going to hit the road and spend some time traveling the world."

"That sounds great," I say. "I'd love to travel the world."

"Here she comes now," says Shirley, hopping down from the trunk and pointing at a truck approaching from a distance.

Babs pulls up in front of the Mustang and jumps out. She's tiny, only up to Shirley's shoulder, with short gray hair and glasses with cool red frames. She's probably older than Shirley, but extremely healthy looking, fit, and toned, with clear skin and bright eyes. I wonder if she's a vegan.

Shirley introduces us all around, and then Babs bends over to check under the hood as the rest of us crowd around behind her. She tinkers around and pokes at a few things, muttering under her breath. Finally she stands up, wiping her hands on the rag that's tucked into her pocket.

"Not good," she says. "Carburetor is shot. Gonna be a few days before I can get the right parts from the city."

Talia groans.

"It's okay, honey," says Shirley. "You all can come back to our house and make some calls. I'm sure you can figure something out with your folks."

Babs looks at Talia. "You been working on this car yourself?"

Talia points at me.

"A buddy and I did most of the work," I say. "Well, he did, anyway."

Babs snorts. "Well, he didn't know what he was doing. You're lucky it's salvageable at all."

"Yeah, well, he was full of unpleasant surprises," I say.

"I guess we can say goodbye to Pride," says Talia. "By the time Mom and Gary find out what's up, we'll be lucky if we don't get locked into Grandma's condo."

"Pride," says Shirley, wistfully. "I haven't been to Pride in years. Remember how much fun we used to have, Babs?"

Babs nods, a distant grin on her face. "I sure do," she says. "Was a different kind of scene back then, that's for sure."

Shirley turns to glance back at the diner. When she looks back at us, she's got a funny look on her face, like she's scheming.

"What do you have planned for the next couple of days, Babs?" she asks.

Babs raises an eyebrow, and a half smile crosses her face. "You're always working an angle, aren't you, Junior?"

Shirley laughs. "Come on," she says. "It'll be fun. It's not like I'll be disappointing our loyal clientele if we shut down for a few days."

"What are you guys talking about?" asks Paige.

"How would you kids like a ride to Toronto?" asks Shirley. "A spur-of-the-moment trip to Pride might be just what the doctor ordered."

CHAPTER SIXTEEN

TALIA

A couple of hours and a carton of ice cream later, the three of us are squeezed into the back of Babs and Shirley's silver pickup truck and on our way to Toronto.

"Toyota Tacoma," Babs says, thumping the steering wheel. "Ask any mechanic: these babies are bulletproof."

I feel like we should be in a horse-drawn carriage, because Babs and Shirley are basically our fairy godmothers: a friend of Babs came and towed our smoking wreck to his garage while Babs packed a weekend bag and Shirley made us all banana splits in the kitchen of their tiny house, just down the street from the diner. It'll be at least eleven before we're in Toronto, but Erin's working until midnight anyway. I sent a text to say we had car trouble and were running late. We didn't call our parents, though, and I still don't know what Mark's going to do with Paige when we get to the city.

But that is not my problem. I have a relationship to save. I'm not going to give up on Erin without a fight, and as much as I adore Paige, I am definitely not available to babysit tonight.

Babs turns on the radio, scans through a few stations featuring classic rock and heavy static, and turns it off again with a grunt. "Well. Last time we went to Toronto for Pride was . . . what year was that, Shirley?"

Shirley has flipped down the visor mirror and is applying bright red lipstick. "Mmm . . ." She smacks her lips together and pushes the mirror back up. "Mid-nineties, must have been. More than twenty years."

"1996," Babs says. "It was the year of the first Dyke March. Remember all the fuss about it? And not knowing if anyone would show up?"

Shirley nods. "'Course, we've been to Pride in Orillia more recently. But that's not anything like Toronto, of course."

Babs continues as if Shirley hasn't spoken. "And the police said we'd have to march on the sidewalks if fewer than a hundred women showed up."

"And did they?" Paige asks. "I mean, more than a hundred?"

"Oh, yes, of course. Lots. Though we were a bit worried because it was pissing rain and it started late—"

"Lesbian time," Shirley interjects. "But it was a great march. A great day."

"Was that the year we went to the Rose after the march?" Babs looks at Shirley. "Our friend Gord was with us that night, and they had that rule—men could only go in the bar if they had a certain number of women with them. And we had to argue with that girl at the door—"

"Who couldn't have been more than twenty—barely old enough to be in the bar herself—"

"How old are you guys anyway?" Paige interrupts.

"Paige!" I elbow her. "That's rude."

Paige looks taken aback. "Why is it rude?"

"It isn't rude at all, darling," Babs says. "I'm sixty-eight. And Shirley is—"

"Younger," Shirley cuts in.

Babs snorts. "Anyway, when we came out in the early seventies, there was no such thing as a lesbian bar. Not really. Wasn't until ten years later that the lesbian scene in Toronto started to take off."

"We made the most of it, though," Shirley says. "Babs was quite the pool shark. Quite the flirt, too."

Babs just laughs.

"How long have you two been together?" I ask.

"Married since it became legal in Ontario. The summer of 2003. Took another two years before it was recognized across the country, but we didn't wait for that . . ." Babs looks at Shirley, like this is a question they always answer in two parts. A routine they have down to a fine art.

"We'd already been waiting long enough," Shirley says. "We've been together almost forty years."

"Wow," Paige says.

I actually have goosebumps. And a lump in my throat. I've just realized I've never actually met a queer couple who've been together a long time. And that's kind of weird, right? I mean— where are they all? They must be out there.

"That's pretty awesome," Mark says.

He's been really quiet. Upset about Darren, I guess, and about the car. I look across at him, catch his eye, and nod. It is so awesome.

"Did you guys go to Pride back then? Like, in the seventies?" I ask.

"I don't think there even was Pride then," Mark says. "Was there?"

"Just getting started, back in those days," Babs says. "Began after the Stonewall Riots."

"There were riots in Toronto?" Mark asks.

"You don't know about Stonewall?" Shirley swivels in her seat to stare at us, and she actually tut-tuts.

"I do," I mutter. The truth is, even though I've heard people mention it—I think there was a movie about it that a lot of queer people boycotted—I don't really know what it was all about.

Shirley wags a finger at us. "That's your history, you know. At least, I assume you two are gay, since you're going to Pride? Or does everyone go nowadays? Are you two actually a couple?"

"God, no! We're cousins," I say.

"We're gay," Mark says.

"Queer," I say, and I think Shirley winces slightly.

"Language is always changing, I suppose, but I swear, my gaydar doesn't work on your generation," she says.

"So what was the deal?" Mark presses. "With the riots?"

It is Babs who replies. "1969," she says. "New York City. The Stonewall Inn was a gay bar, and the riots were when people fought back against the police who were harassing and arresting them. You oughta look it up. Same thing happened in Toronto in the early eighties, remember that, Shirley? After the bathhouse raids?"

"What's a bathhouse?" Paige asks.

There is a moment's awkward silence.

"'Course, things are better now," Babs says, changing the subject. "Things have changed. But you should know your history. It's important." She shakes her head, meeting our eyes in the rearview mirror. "Can't take rights for granted."

"So what are you kids planning to do when we get to Toronto?" Shirley asks.

"I'm meeting up with someone," I say. "Down at Church and Wellesley."

"Girlfriend?" Shirley asks.

"Well. Partner. Or maybe ex. I'm not sure. We were together all through high school, practically, but now . . ." I make a face. "That's kind of why I need to get to Toronto. To sort it all out."

"Erin's nonbinary," Paige says, outing Erin just like I've told her not to. Though I guess it's probably okay in this situation. "So they're not a girlfriend or boyfriend, exactly. But not just a friend either."

Babs nods. "Can't say I've ever felt much like a girl or a boy myself. Didn't have a word for that when we were younger."

"Well, *butch*," Shirley says.

"That's how you identify?" I ask. "As butch?"

"Mmm." Babs reaches across and puts her hand on Shirley's knee. "Butch and femme. Out of fashion these days, I suppose."

"No, it's cool." I don't know anyone my age who IDs that way, but I think it's kind of awesome, actually. "But . . . well, *butch* means butch woman, right? Or butch lesbian? So it's not the same as being nonbinary. I guess it could be genderqueer, maybe?" I look at Mark for help, but he just shrugs.

Babs nods. "Woman or man, that was all there was back in those days. Far as I knew at the time, anyway. If I were a young person now, I'd probably . . ." She shrugs. "Well, I don't know exactly. I don't really know. More choices now than we had."

I almost say that none of this is about choice, exactly—but then I hold back, because I think I understand what she is saying.

"I think it's just great that you kids aren't letting anyone put you in boxes where you don't fit, I'll say that much," Shirley puts in. "If the old words and ideas don't work, why shouldn't you invent new ones?"

"I know, right?" I shrug. "It gets complicated, though. Like at school. People want you just to pick a label and stick with it, and if you're still trying to figure it out or, like, if it changes, then people act like you're just making stuff up or attention seeking or something."

"What about you, Mark?" Shirley says.

"Me?" He frowns. "Uh, I'm just gay."

She laughs. "Sorry, I meant what about you when we get to the city? You and your sister got plans?"

"Oh. Right. I haven't really thought it all through yet," Mark says. "We need to find somewhere to spend the night, I guess. I could drop Paige off with my mom, but . . ."

Talia jumps in. "Our grandma is in the hospital, so they've kind of got enough going on . . ."

Shirley and Babs exchange a long look, and I know what they're going to say before they even say it.

"We're staying at a friend's place," Shirley says. "I'm sure they wouldn't mind if you came along. You might be on the couch, but it's going to be pretty late by the time we get to the city."

Mark grins. "Thanks so much," he says. "You guys are the best."

The way he always lands on his feet is unbelievable. I bet he's already scheming about how to leave Paige with them so he can go out partying.

"Can you drop me off downtown?" I say. "Near a subway stop?"

"We'll take to you to your friend," Shirley says. "I don't like the idea of you wandering around the city on your own."

I let out a breath of relief. Erin explained the subways, but I've never actually been on one, and I was pretty nervous about finding my way. "Thanks," I say. "Mark's right: you guys really are the best."

I almost tell them they're like fairy godmothers but decide against it.

———

It is eleven-thirty when we finally arrive at the Village. I am a little worried that they might all want to come in and meet Erin, but luckily the street seems to be closed to traffic and there is nowhere nearby to park, so I just thank Babs and Shirley profusely, and I hop out and promise to text Mark in the morning. Then I wave as they drive away.

I let out a long breath, and stand alone, taking deep breaths of the warm evening air, the warm, so-queer-it's-practically-shimmering-with-rainbows evening air.

Even this late at night, Church and Wellesley—on the Friday night of Pride weekend—are packed with people: rowdy groups spilling off patios and onto the sidewalks, cute young guys strolling along holding hands, older couples walking arm in arm. A couple of drag queens serve drinks at one open-fronted bar. Two ponytailed Asian girls who look about my age lean against the wall of a building, deep in conversation. A fat black woman in an ankle-length baby blue dress walks a Rottweiler puppy with a studded collar. In the middle of the intersection, a man in a top hat and blue eyeshadow performs mime with a rose held between his teeth. I can't stop staring. Someone bumps into me and apologizes, and I turn: short hair, freckles, brown eyes, an adorable grin. She's wearing a T-shirt that says *Queer AF,* sleeves rolled up to show off distinct biceps and brightly colored tattoos on the inside of both forearms. Birds, I think . . .

I stutter something back, feeling myself blush, but she's already walking on past.

Wow. Maybe Erin's right: I do need to get out more.

Erin. Right. Where is Erin? I pull out my phone and enter the name of the coffee shop into the map app. The blue dot that is me pops up right beside the dot that is the coffee shop: I'm standing right in front of it.

And I'm suddenly scared to go in.

CHAPTER SEVENTEEN

MARK

When we finally pull up to the house in Greektown, it's after midnight. It occurs to me that Mom would be totally pissed if she knew that I was letting Paige stay up this late, but Paige is wide awake and as excited as I am, so I don't overthink it.

The truck has to circle the block a few times to find a parking spot that's big enough, but finally we come upon a bunch of screaming young people climbing into a minivan. It pulls away from the curb, and Babs slides the Tacoma into place and turns off the engine.

"Toronto is exciting," says Paige as we hop out of the truck. On the sidewalk, I stretch out my tight muscles and bounce on my feet a bit, happy to be out of the cramped backseat.

"You can say that again," I say. We're on a street lined with brick houses. They're narrow, but tall, with ornate curved windows and fancy trim dangling like icicles from the peaked roof. Laughter and the sound of clinking bottles drift out at us from backyards.

I grab my bag and hand Paige her backpack, and we follow Babs and Shirley up the walkway to one of the houses. On a street full of nice homes, this one is particularly impressive. The small front yard is full of impeccably groomed flowerbeds, and the railings on the front steps have been freshly painted. Paige and I follow the women up the steps and stand behind them as Shirley rings the doorbell beside a gorgeous heavy wooden door that's accented with an elaborate stained glass window.

"Nice place," I say with a whistle.

"No kidding," says Shirley. "The boys have always had great taste. When I first met them, they were broke as a joke, just like the rest of us, but they had the coolest little apartment, full of awesome thrift store furniture and artwork they'd picked up from friends."

The door swings open and a very handsome black man stands on the other side. He's bald, with expensive-looking wire-framed glasses, and is very nicely dressed in gray khakis and a white button-up, with a navy blue velvet blazer. He has a bottle of beer in one hand, and he steps back with a look of distaste when he sees us.

"Well, look what the cat dragged in," he says.

I wonder if there's some unresolved drama between this guy and Shirley and Babs, but then a wide grin crosses his face and he reaches out to give them both huge hugs.

"It's so great to see you girls," he says. "This is so exciting. A last-minute trip to the big city for the country mice." He glances past them at me and Paige. "And who have we here?"

"This is Mark and Paige," says Babs. "They had some car trouble on their way to the city and found their way to the diner."

"Oh, lord," he says, shaking our hands. "Don't tell me you let Shirley cook for you."

Shirley laughs. "This," she tells us, "is the incomparable Derek Young."

From the depths of the house, someone hollers excitedly. "Are they here? Is it them?"

From behind Derek comes another man. He's white, very tall, with high cheekbones and a perfect coif of thick gray hair. He's dressed much more flamboyantly than Derek, with a brightly patterned silk shirt over slim red pants. He stops in the doorway and shakes his head as he stares out at Babs and Shirley. He lifts a fist to his mouth and bites on a knuckle, as if he's overcome with emotion.

"Oh, come here, you old softie," says Shirley. She reaches out and gives him a long embrace. When they pull back, I realize that he's crying a little bit, and Shirley's face is also wet.

Babs leans in to me and Paige. "They have a very long history," she whispers. "They've been through a lot together."

"We have indeed, Barbara," says the man. He leans in and gives her a kiss on the cheek. "You've been taking care of my Shirley?"

"As always," says Babs.

"Mark, Paige," says Shirley. "This is Kenny Grisham, Derek's husband."

Kenny puts his arm around Derek and they share a quick peck on the lips. "Please, come in! I can't believe you're still out on the porch. There are a few people in the backyard. We have a full house for Pride."

We follow the men inside and down a long hallway. The inside of the house is even nicer than the outside. I glance through a wide archway and spot a room with a wall full of books and elegant, expensive-looking furniture arranged around a glass coffee table on a large oriental rug. There's even a baby grand piano in one corner.

"Holy shit," I whisper. "This place is unbelievable."

"They do all right for themselves," says Babs. "Kenny is a production designer in the film industry, and Derek is a lawyer."

In the kitchen at the back of the house, a large room with beamed ceilings and stainless steel, we stop and drop our bags into chairs. Derek pours some wine for Shirley and finds a beer for Babs, and offers Paige and me sodas.

"Do we have to go back to Grandma's condo?" Paige asks as we walk through a set of French doors into the backyard.

There's a fire pit burning on a stone terrace, and about a half dozen people are sitting around it. Most of them are older, but I notice a good-looking young guy, not much older than I am, in conversation with a woman on the other side of the fire. A few of the guests know Babs and Shirley, and there are more heartfelt hugs and introductions, and then Paige and I stand off to the side, shyly sipping our sodas.

Kenny comes up beside us. "Poor young things," he says. "This must be as boring as it gets." He calls across the fire: "Jeremy! Come meet our new friends!"

The good-looking guy excuses himself from the conversation and comes over to us, smiling.

"Mark, Paige," says Kenny, "meet my nephew Jeremy. He's in town for Pride, just like you two."

I feel a thrill of expectation as I shake Jeremy's hand. *He's in town for Pride.* Does this mean he's gay?

"You going out tonight?" Jeremy asks me. "Downtown?"

"Oh," I say, "I hadn't, um, I hadn't really thought that far ahead."

He laughs. "Well, you're welcome to join me. I'm supposed to meet up with some of my friends in a little while."

"That sounds awesome," I say. I glance at Paige, who is looking up at me expectantly. I immediately wonder if I can persuade Babs and Shirley to take care of her for the night. I know exactly what Talia would think of that plan, but, fortunately, she isn't around to rain on my parade.

Shirley sees us chatting and comes over to us. "We should think about getting you to bed," she says to Paige. "I'd guess it's way past your bedtime."

"I have one of the basement bedrooms set up for these guys already," says Kenny. "You guys mind sharing a room for the night? Bunk beds?"

"That sounds great," I say, trying to keep my face calm. This might fall into place perfectly.

"You want to call your mom first?" Shirley asks Paige. "Tell her you made it to the city all right?"

"Oh, she doesn't know we're here," says Paige.

A look crosses between Shirley and Kenny. "Your mother doesn't know about your trip to the city?" asks Shirley.

"That's not exactly—" I begin, but Paige is too quick for me.

"Mark was trying to sneak away," she says, "but Talia and I caught him, and he agreed to come with us if we wouldn't tell our folks. They wouldn't like this."

I'm struggling to come up with a good excuse when I catch Jeremy's amused face from behind Shirley's shoulder. He gives me a quick wink, and I lose all ability to think on the spot.

"I'm sorry," says Kenny. "You know we're always happy to find room for guests, Shirley, but this makes me very uncomfortable."

"Yes, of course," says Shirley. "I totally understand."

"What's going on?" asks Derek, approaching.

Shirley fills him in, and I open my mouth to apologize, but he lifts a finger to shush me. "We've all been there, guys," he says. "We've all had to lie and make excuses. Without little white lies, I never would have found my way into my first gay bar."

"It's true, honey," says Kenny, "and if it were just Mark, I could justify it, but Paige is—how old are you, sweetie?"

"Ten," says Paige.

"Ten," repeats Kenny. "We can't do it. I'm sorry, guys."

"What about this," says Derek. "Why don't you call your mother and explain what's going on. See what she says. Maybe she'll give you permission to stay."

I already know that's not going to happen, but I know that arguing is pointless.

"Okay," I say, miserably. "I'll call her now."

I step to the shadows at the back of the yard before calling. It's already rung three times by the time I remember how late it is.

"Mark?" she asks breathlessly, picking up. "What's the matter?"

"Nothing's the matter," I say. I realize I've woken her up. Of course I have; it's half past twelve. "I'm just—I just."

"Where are you?" she asks. "What's that noise in the background."

"It's kind of a—it's a party," I say.

"At the cottage? Is Paige there? What is going on?"

"Mom, listen, I'll explain." I take a breath, and then unload the whole story. When I'm done, I stop, waiting for her to say something.

There's a long pause. Then, "What's the address?" she asks. I can tell from the tone of her voice that she is not in a forgiving mood.

"I'll send you a text," I say.

"I'll be there ASAP," she says. "Wait on the front step."

She hangs up before I can respond.

Paige and I gather our things and say our goodbyes to everyone.

"It's probably for the best," says Babs.

I nod, miserably.

"You sure you don't want us to sit on the porch with you?" asks Shirley.

"No," I say. "Thanks. Mom will just have a million questions."

"We don't mind," she says.

"Shirley, the kid doesn't want to be embarrassed any more than he already is," says Babs.

We hug them goodbye, and promise to get in touch when things are sorted out. We'll have to figure out what to do with the car, and Babs promises to help us out, so at least there's that.

Paige is still wide awake as we sit on the front step, but neither of us says anything as we wait for Mom. Then I see her rental car come around the corner, a block away. She's going slow, reading the numbers on the houses, and Paige stands to wave for her.

"Pssst," says a voice in the shadows beside me. I turn to see Jeremy coming around the side of the house. He smiles mischievously, and he tilts his head toward the opposite end of the street. "Bus is leaving in three minutes. We'd better run if we want to catch it."

I turn to look at Paige, who's walking down the steps toward Mom, who has pulled up and double parked, waiting for us.

"Paige," I say. She turns and I shove my bag at her. "Please," I say. "I will totally owe you one."

She gives me a long, hard look, then a small nod as she grabs my bag.

The passenger-side window rolls down, and I hear my mother yelling for me, but her voice soon recedes in the distance as I race after Jeremy into the night.

CHAPTER EIGHTEEN
TALIA

Erin is standing in the middle of the room, in a small cluster of people with colorful hair and clothes that are way cooler than my straight-from-cottage-country jeans and hoodie. Erin's head is thrown back, their mouth open in a tooth-flashing laugh, totally at ease in this strange new place.

Some people just naturally gravitate to center stage. That's always been Erin: comfortable in the limelight.

Everyone at school knew us as Erin-and-Talia. Always Erin-and-Talia. It would sound wrong saying it the other way around: Talia-and-Erin. Like saying "fries and a burger," instead of "a burger and fries."

And now, standing on the sidewalk, looking in through the window at the crowded cafe, I feel it more strongly than ever: Erin's the sun and I'm some dumb little exoplanet caught in its orbit.

I push the door open, blow out a breath, and force myself to step inside: music, voices, clinking glasses, air just a little too warm and too humid for comfort. I make my way through the crowds, toward Erin, and my heart is racing. Part of me had thought Erin might be . . . well, more alone, here in this new city. But they look just as confident, just as at ease, as always. And I feel totally anxious and insecure.

"Erin?" I call, hanging back a little.

Erin whirls around at my voice. "TALIA!"

And my doubts recede as I'm pulled in tight for a quick, hard, familiar hug. "I've missed you so much," I say, my words muffled against Erin's shoulder.

Erin releases me and holds me at arm's length for a second, studying my face. "I've missed you too. Seriously. SO much!"

The cluster of people standing nearby slowly come into focus. There are three of them. All staring at me.

"You must be Talia," one says. He's my height and slender, with light brown skin, a short dark goatee, and a double-pierced eyebrow. He looks at least a couple of years older than us, and wears a T-shirt that says *Dissent is Patriotic*.

"Sorry," Erin says. "Um. Talia, this is Jack. And—" They turn to two girls with hair dyed in bright rainbow shades. "—Kade and Brooke."

I push back a flicker of jealousy. "Hi. Um, I love your hair. Did you . . . I mean, is that for Pride weekend?"

"Yeah." It's Brooke who answers. She's tall and curvy, wearing a very short black dress that shows a lot of creamy white skin and tattooed cleavage. "Two days ago mine was all pink, and Kade's was blond."

Kade wrinkles her nose and giggles. "So boring!" She's slender, with huge black-lined eyes and pink lipstick, and looks like an anime cosplayer.

"That's awesome." Brooke and Kade both have the kind of thick straight hair that looks good in any style. Hair that can actually *have* styles. Mine's a mess of frizzy curls, and if I tried doing what they've done, the different-colored streaks would all end up mixed together and look dumb. I don't usually care about things like this, but I can't help it: it's almost midnight, and it's been a really long day, and I really want to be alone with Erin. "So, you guys all live in Toronto?"

"Born and bred," Brooke says. "Jack's at U of T. Kade and I go to Sheridan."

Maybe they're a couple? Or maybe I just want them to be, because the idea of Erin spending all their time surrounded by cute single girls is making me feel a little more uncomfortable than it should.

A: We are not even together, probably, maybe.

And B: If we were together, I should trust Erin.

I hate the idea of being jealous, but Erin's words still echo in my head: *We've talked about having a more open relationship, right? Maybe this is a good time to try it?*

What if they already are? With Brooke or Kade? Or both?

Erin glances at their watch. "Give me five minutes. I'll just go clean up in the back and we'll get out of here. Okay?"

I nod.

"You can hang with these guys," Erin says, and they disappear behind the counter, whisking a few empty mugs from tables as they go.

I turn back to Jack, Kade, and Brooke. "So, um, what are you guys studying?"

"Film," Brooke says. "Kade and I are in the same program. Jack's pre-med."

"Oh, wow. Cool." I sound twelve. "I'm going to U Vic in the fall."

"I know," Jack says. "Erin's talked about you lots."

"Oh. Um, really?"

"Yeah, of course. Sounds like you guys did a lot of organizing at your high school. Starting a GSA? That's pretty awesome."

"Erin told you about that?"

He nods. "I was at a private Christian school in Alberta. Our administration basically looked for opportunities to fight any remotely progressive thing anyone tried to do."

"Ouch. Were you out in high school?" I realize I've just assumed he is gay. Is that totally uncool? I mean, we're in the Village and talking about GSAs . . ."

"Yes and no." He shakes his head. "It's complicated."

"Sorry, I didn't mean to . . ."

158

"No, it's cool. Anyway, U of T is great. Toronto's great."

Brooke nods. "Yeah, it is. How come you picked U Vic? Did you just want to stay closer to home for first year? I mean, I get that. My mom's just in Burlington, so I can go home for a weekend if I want to."

Kade giggles. "Not that she ever wants to."

I feel stupider and younger by the second. Why didn't I push Dad a bit more? Maybe he couldn't afford for me to go to school away from home, but I could've moved to Toronto with Erin and gotten a job. I could've gone to school part-time. Or worked in Toronto for a year and saved some money. At least Erin and I would've stayed together. Maybe Brooke is right and I was just scared to leave home . . .

"Okay!" Erin reappears beside me and grabs my arm. "Ready to go?"

I nod.

"Cool." They turn to the others. "See you all tomorrow? Dyke March, right?"

All three of them nod. "I'll text you," Jack says.

And we're heading out the door and into the night.

———————

I wanted to be alone with Erin, but now that I am, I feel suddenly shy. I sneak a sideways glance at them—same short brown hair, same thin face and wide grin—but even though it's only been a couple of weeks, everything feels different. Awkward. Like we don't know each other anymore.

"How's your grandmother?"

"She'll be okay. Do you like Toronto? And your job?"

"Yeah, it's great."

In a minute we'll be talking about the weather. I find myself blinking back tears.

"Erin?"

"Yeah?"

"Are you . . . are we . . . um . . ." I gulp back a sob. "Are we still a couple? Sort of? Or . . ."

Erin stops walking and turns to me. "I never wanted to break up, Talia. You know that."

"But you left. You took this job; you decided to go to Toronto." I drop my eyes, thinking, again, of Brooke and Kade. "You wanted to see other people."

Erin doesn't answer right away. We're standing in front of a bar, and people and laughter are spilling out onto the street. The loud beat of the music thuds in my chest and it feels like my own heart is drumming out of rhythm. When I look up, I find Erin's eyes—hazel, with green flecks—waiting to meet mine. "Talia. I just. We've been together since we were sixteen. That's . . . well, it's a long time."

"You're tired of me?"

"No! God, Talia. Of course not. You're my best friend. Before

I left Victoria, I couldn't even imagine getting through a day without you."

"But now you can? It's not so bad?"

Erin holds my gaze for a long moment, and then looks away, eyes shining. *Are those actually tears?* "It's not that, Talia. I miss you all the time. Something funny happens, or something weird, or sad . . . I find myself thinking about how I'll turn it into a story to tell you. And then I remember that you're not here, and I miss you all over again. I mean, this happens dozens of times every day."

I nod. "Me too," I say. "Me too."

"But if we stay together . . . I mean, we were practically the only queer kids in our school. We ended up together because there was no one else. Maybe you wouldn't even have picked me, you know?"

"I would've," I say. "I still would. I *do*."

There's a silence, and then Erin says, "I don't want to break up. But I don't want to never be with anyone else, you know?"

I suck in my breath. I don't want to know. But I have to ask. "Are you seeing someone? Already?"

Erin's hesitation is an answer in itself.

"Brooke?" I ask. "Kade?"

"No, no. They're a couple; couldn't you tell? The matching hair?"

I shrug. "I wasn't sure."

"Anyway. I'm not exactly seeing anyone. But I've been spending a lot of time with Jack."

"Jack? Seriously?"

"Yeah." Erin's eyes narrow: a danger sign. "Why *not* Jack?"

"Because he's . . . a guy. I always thought, if you got involved with someone else . . ." I shrug. "I don't know. I'm an idiot."

"I've always said I'm pan," Erin says.

"I know. I know." It's true. I don't know why I'm so surprised.

"Anyway." Erin shrugs. "Nothing's happened. I'm not sure where it's going. Or if it's going anywhere. But we talk. Like, a lot. There's some chemistry there, I guess. Plus he's trans, too. He gets some of what I'm going through. What I'm trying to figure out. He even identified as nonbinary for a while before he decided that being a guy actually made more sense for him. That it was a better fit."

"He's trans?" My mind skips ahead. "Wait, you're not going to . . ."

"Do the same thing? No. At least, I don't think so." Erin looks at me. "Why? Would it be a problem for you if I was?"

"No. Of course not." I'm taken aback, though: Erin's never really talked about this before.

"Are you sure?"

I think about it for a moment. It'd be weird, in a way, having people see us and think we're a het couple. But if I just think about me and Erin, and not about how other people see us or don't see us . . . Erin is still Erin—whatever pronouns they use, however they identify, however they are seen in the world. I guess it's kind of self-centered to be making this about me at all.

"I wouldn't care," I say. "I love you. I just want you to be happy."

"I am happy. I've missed you, but I've been really happy. I was so ready to leave Victoria, you know? I didn't even realize how ready I was. But it is so good to be in . . . well, a bigger world. To meet new people." Erin reaches out and takes my hand. Their fingers lace between mine, so smoothly, so easily, like they have a thousand times before. "Oh my god, Talia. It is so good to see you."

"It's good to see you, too," I say, but I'm holding back tears. Erin's only known Jack for a couple of weeks and they've talked about stuff that Erin has never talked about with me. I wish I wasn't jealous—but I am.

"Toronto and Victoria aren't all that far apart, you know? I'll be home at Christmas," Erin says. "And we can Skype. Text . . ."

I stare down at our hands. Erin's long fingers and square nails, my paler skin and brightly colored bracelets. "I love you," I say. "But I can't do this. I can't be with you if you want to be with other people as well."

Erin doesn't answer.

I pull my hand away.

And right there, in the heart of the queer village, on the cusp of Pride weekend, I burst into tears.

"I love you," Erin whispers. "Talia, I love you so much."

I want that to be enough.

More than anything, I wish that was enough.

CHAPTER NINETEEN

MARK

This is it. This is the night I've been hoping for, the downtown Toronto Gay Pride super night. Warm night air, the faintest hint of breeze keeping the humidity from being too gross.

Then there's Jeremy, the cute boy by my side. No, scratch that—cute doesn't do him justice. He's handsome, if I've ever seen handsome, and now he's leading me into the night, in a city that I've never seen in this light before.

Jeremy's walk exudes confidence, an easy swagger that makes me assume he's an athlete—something powerful by the looks of his legs, his muscular frame.

"You play football?" I ask.

"Ballet," he says, turning to smile at me. "Football is for lightweights. Ballet takes real strength."

"No kidding?" I say, half to myself.

"Here we are," he says as we turn a corner and come up on a subway stop.

"You really know your way around," I say as we trot down the stairs to the platform.

"I've spent my whole life in Toronto," he says.

"I thought you were just crashing here for Pride," I say, confused.

"I live with my folks in Brampton," he says. "I'm just crashing with Kenny and Derek for the weekend because they live so close to downtown."

"Toronto's a hell of a lot bigger than Halifax," I say.

He laughs. "So I've heard. I also just like hanging out with the uncles during Pride. They always have a lot of cool friends around. It's kind of like hanging out at a queer history lesson sometimes, but they're a lot of fun. They like to see the younger generation heading out and having a good time. Taking up the gay pride flag, so to speak."

The train rumbles toward us with a whoosh of hot air, and we climb onto the half-empty train.

"Does it run all night?" I ask.

"Just until one thirty," he says. "This is probably the last train." He pulls out his phone. "I'm gonna text my friends and find out where they are."

With great reluctance, I pull my own phone out of my pocket. As expected, there's a series of furious texts from my mother, culminating in: Do I need to call the cops?!?!

I sigh and text her back. No. I'm hanging out in town for Pride weekend—won't drink or do drugs, promise. I hit send, then compose another text. I know I'm in really big trouble. I'll take my punishment without complaining. But I've been dreaming about this forever. I'll never be seventeen again.

"I am in some seriously deep shit," I tell Jeremy as I slide my phone back into my pocket without waiting for her response. "You think your uncles would mind if I crash there this weekend?"

He smiles and shakes his head. "No problem; they have lots of space. I think they've been a refuge for wayward teens more than once."

"Is that me?" I ask, slipping seamlessly into flirt mode. "A wayward boy?"

"That remains to be seen," he says with a wink. He stands, grabbing onto a pole as the train slows down. "This is our stop."

We climb out of the train and follow the crowd up the stairs and onto the street. I feel like Dorothy must have felt when she landed in Oz. Music pumps through the air, and everywhere I look there are people laughing and dancing and making out. Some people are dressed simply, like Jeremy and me, but there are loads of pride flags draped over shoulders, and wild costumes and glow bracelets and parasols. It reminds me of Halifax Pride, only bigger. Much, much bigger.

"Holy shit," I say. "There are so many people."

"Welcome to Toronto Pride," says Jeremy. "Come on, let's go meet my friends."

We wend our way through the crowd, crossing the street and cutting through a small park. On one end a stage has been set up, and a DJ is spinning something happy and upbeat. People are dancing in front of the stage, and as I watch, a tiny guy wearing a gold speedo, a pair of angel wings, and not much else, climbs up onto the front of the stage and starts to lead the crowd in a chant.

"There is no one alive who is youer than you!" he yells into the crowd. A few people near the front yell it back at him.

"I think that's a Dr. Seuss quote," I yell to Jeremy, who's just in front of me.

"Of course it is," he says. He turns around and grabs me by the hand. I feel a flutter down my spine, but then I realize he's only trying to pull me out of the park and away from the dancing maniacs. We step back onto the sidewalk and he lets go, without any pretense. "This way," he says.

We walk for a couple of blocks, moving away from the center of activity, although there are still people everywhere. We stop at a busy, brightly lit corner flanked by tall windows. It's a twenty-four-hour diner, and inside, I can see tables crammed with excited revelers. We press through the clusters of people standing outside smoking cigarettes and weed, and I follow Jeremy through the jingling door into the diner.

We stand in the entry for a moment as he scans the crowd, then his face lights up. "There they are," he says, pointing.

His friends are at a booth in the corner, two girls on one side, two guys on the other. The girls are hovering over a phone, looking at something, and on the other side of the booth, a really small guy is half asleep on the other guy's much taller shoulder.

"Oh look," says Jeremy, as we approach. "It's couples corner."

They all turn to us and their faces brighten.

"Jeremy!" the taller guy says. "Where the hell have you been?"

"I was at my uncle's place," says Jeremy. "Time kind of got away from me. Have you guys eaten yet?"

"We've ordered, but the food isn't here yet," says one of the girls. "It's pretty crazy in here."

"You hungry?" Jeremy asks me.

I realize that I am, in fact, starving. I haven't eaten since we got to the city, other than a bag of peanuts that Shirley passed around in the truck. "Totally," I say.

Jeremy slides into the booth and I slide in across from him, next to the girls.

"Guys, this is Mark," says Jeremy. "He's in town from Halifax. His first Pride."

"My first Toronto Pride," I correct.

"Ooh, Halifax," says the taller guy. "Did you hitch a ride with a bunch of shirtless sailors?"

"I wish," I say, which earns me a wink from him.

"Everything's a porno setup for you, isn't it, Dax?" asks the girl sitting up against the window. She's got super short, bleached blond hair, and a super wide mouth accentuated with bright red lipstick.

"Pretty much," says Dax, shrugging. The guy who's curled into him opens his eyes halfway and lets out a short, abrupt laugh, then lets out a contented sigh and nestles farther into Dax.

"I'm Betty," says the bleach-haired girl as she reaches around the other girl to give me a firm handshake.

"Parul," says the other girl with a reserved smile and a slight nod of the head to me. She's gorgeous, dark skinned, with wide eyes and thick, glossy hair that's pulled into two braids.

"What's up with him?" asks Jeremy, gesturing to the small guy who is now lightly snoring on Dax's chest.

Dax rolls his eyes. "Too much partying for Clem," he says. "By the time we met up, he'd already been downtown for hours, drinking and doing god knows what. He'll pay for it tomorrow."

The waitress arrives, and I quickly scan the menu before ordering a cheeseburger and onion rings. Jeremy orders a falafel wrap.

"So what's the plan for the rest of the night?" Jeremy asks.

"This is it for us," says Betty. "We have to reserve our energy for tomorrow."

Dax nods. "I won't be able to dance till my ass falls off unless I get a good night's sleep. Besides, I have to get Little Lord Fauntleroy here home to bed."

"You guys going to the Dyke March tomorrow?" asks Jeremy.

"Totally," says Betty.

"I have to work," says Parul miserably.

Betty leans over and gives her a kiss on the cheek. "Don't worry, babe, we'll be waiting for you when you get off work. It'll be epic."

Parul nods. "Yeah. I know. I just hate to miss it. The big parade is so corporate; I don't identify with it the same way."

"I know, sweetie," says Betty. "I'll make it up to you." She teases Parul's hair and Parul smiles sheepishly before giving in to it and twisting in her seat to give Betty a genuine kiss that lingers for just a few seconds.

"Jesus, get a room," says Dax.

"I'm sorry," says Betty, "I must be thinking of someone else who full on made out with his boyfriend on one of the DJ stages last year."

"Shhhh!" says Dax, pointing dramatically at Clem, who chooses this moment to wake up, sitting upright with a dazed expression on his face.

"Who's making out?" he asks, rubbing his eyes. He turns and looks at me. "Who the hell are you?"

The rest of us burst into laughter just as the food starts to arrive at the table. Clem immediately digs into Dax's plate of food.

"You said you didn't want to eat anything," says Dax, only jokingly annoyed.

Their pretend argument draws in Betty and Parul, and soon they're trading stories about their afternoon and evening downtown.

"We'll grab a cab back to Derek and Kenny's after this," says Jeremy, smiling across the table at me. "Sorry it was kind of a bust tonight. I promise we'll make up for it tomorrow. It's going to be an epic party."

"It wasn't a bust at all," I say. "Seriously, I'm just so happy to be here instead of in my grandmother's sad condo with my mom and sister and uncle."

At mention of Grandma, I feel a wave of guilt pass over me. I didn't even bother to ask Mom how she was doing. It's too late right now, but I resolve to check in with her tomorrow to find out how things are going, and to let her know that I'm okay. I'm not going to budge on attending Pride, though. I have the feeling that tonight is just a small teaser for what's to come tomorrow.

I glance across the table at Jeremy, who's listening to a dramatic and hilarious story that Dax is telling. Something about him hits me somewhere deep, not like Darren. Not like Jareth, even at the start.

Jareth and I are a couple, or *were* a couple, I guess, although I realize that I still haven't really articulated to him that it is over. It wasn't like this, though. It wasn't like Betty and Parul, or Derek and Kenny, or Shirley and Babs. It was really just something fun, something easy. I get an uneasy feeling suddenly, thinking about how Jareth saw our relationship. How differently he viewed things, compared with me.

Jeremy catches my eye across the table, and suddenly I feel a foot tap against mine, the quick slide of his toe up against my ankle, rubbing up and down, just a couple of times before dropping away. A signal of some kind, I'm sure.

I saw the excitement and anticipation in Talia's eyes when we dropped her off at Erin's place. I've never felt that before, but now, looking across at Jeremy, I wonder if I could.

CHAPTER TWENTY
TALIA

I open my eyes. We must have slept in: bright sunlight is streaming in through Erin's bedroom window and I can hear the sounds of people moving around in the kitchen. It's all of ten feet away: this whole apartment is smaller than my bedroom back home.

Erin's head is on my shoulder, their hair tickling my neck. It's hot in here, and I'm sticky with sweat and need a shower. I wriggle my arm free, roll over, and look at the clock. Ten thirty. We stayed up really late, talking and talking and talking. And crying. There was a lot of crying, mostly on my part.

I feel totally emotionally wrung out.

And even after all that, I'm still not sure where we stand. I mean, it seemed like we were breaking up, and then we weren't, and then ended up in bed together . . . just like before Erin left Victoria. We go around in circles, hurting each other, neither of us having the guts to actually end it. Neither of us wanting it to be over.

The apartment door bangs closed and everything is quiet. Their brother and his partner must've left. They got in after us last night, so I haven't even met them—which is fine by me. I don't have the energy to deal with people this morning. I wonder, suddenly, how Mark and Paige are doing and where they are right now.

Beside me, Erin murmurs something and rolls over, then sits up abruptly. "Whassa time?"

"Eleven. What time is the Dyke March?"

Erin swings their legs over the edge of the bed, pulls on a pair of boxers and a T-shirt, and stands up. "Starts at two, but I told people I'd meet them at one. Is that okay? I kind of made plans before I knew you were going to be in town."

"Yeah, fine." Though they could've cancelled the plans, right? If Erin had come back to Victoria unexpectedly, I'd have canceled my plans (if I'd actually made any, which I probably wouldn't have). When Erin was there, I didn't feel like I needed a lot of other friends. And after they left, the last thing I felt like doing was seeing people.

"Coffee?" Erin asks. "My brother probably left a pot."

The kitchen is a little nook at one end of the living room. Erin fills two mugs from a stainless steel carafe and carries them out onto the tiny balcony. "Check out the view."

I peer over the railing. There's another building right across from ours, and at least half the balconies are flying rainbow flags. Down the street, less than a block away, I can see the crowds gathering on Church Street. The air is warm and the sun is shining down, making everything seem to glow. "Where does the march begin?"

Erin points. "Maybe six or eight blocks that way. Then it comes right down Church Street, through the Village, and to this park just a couple of blocks south of here."

I sit down and sip my coffee, and for some reason, my eyes are stinging and I'm suddenly holding back tears. It's not even about Erin, for once: it's all the people down there on the street, and the rainbow flags on the balconies. Maybe it's even about Mark and about Shirley and Babs and their stories about the Stonewall riots and queer life back in the '70s and '80s, and the people in the coffee shop last night, and even Brooke and Kade and Jack . . .

I've talked to more queer people in the past twenty-four hours than I have in my entire life. This sounds stupid, but I don't think I quite grasped that there was this huge community out there. I mean, Erin and I worked our asses off to get our GSA going, and after three years, there were still only six other members, and half of them were straight. But look at all those people down there on Church Street: some of them must've been the only queer kid in their school, or maybe they grew up in a small town where no one was out, or in a super-religious family, or even in another country where it wasn't even legal to be gay . . . and they've all made their way here. They've all come here from somewhere.

There's a lump in my throat and tears in my eyes and a feeling I can't describe swelling in my chest. I'm a part of this. These are my people, this is my community. I may not know exactly how I identify or whatever, but I'm pretty sure that whatever I am, there's a place for me under this great big queer rainbow.

I lean over the balcony and surreptitiously wipe my eyes. "Lots of people out there already," I say.

"It's crazy," Erin says. "Isn't it?"

I nod. "In a good way. Yeah. Are you . . . I guess you're probably used to it? All this . . ." I wave my arm. "Well, all this."

"It's only been two weeks."

Has it really? Two weeks since we were sitting on my bed, fighting, crying? Two weeks since Erin left?

"It feels like longer," I say.

———

We meet up with Erin's friends as planned, at Church and Charles, where the Dyke March will begin. Brooke and Kade and Jack, as well as a few other people whose names I instantly forget: two guys with blond hair and matching unbuttoned Hawaiian shirts, a topless girl in a miniskirt and fishnets with black electrical tape over her nipples, and a girl with a dark ponytail who reminds me of Mariana, and who, to my relief, is dressed like me: denim shorts and a T-shirt. I feel rather boring in this crowd.

Maybe I should trade the navy blue bandana for a rainbow one.

Maybe I don't actually care.

Already the groups are getting lined up on the street: Erin points them out like they're my tour guide. "There's Black Lives Matter!"

I turn to look, reading the T-shirts people are wearing and the signs they are holding as we walk past: *Black Lives Matter. Say Her Name. No Pride in Policing. Stop Trans Murders.* One woman—tall, with long braids—has a small boy with her, maybe three or four years old. His sign dangles at his side: *My Life Matters.*

"Oh, and Dykes on Bikes. It's traditional for them to lead off the march," Erin says.

"I know," I say, eyeing the motorcycles and their riders. "Same in Victoria, right? At Pride?" We marched together last year, with the GSA.

"Right," Erin says. "I don't know why we never had a Dyke March in Victoria."

"Well, Victoria's a lot smaller. But I like our Pride Parade." I feel defensive all of a sudden. Just because Toronto is bigger doesn't mean it's better. Though it's not just bigger: it's way more diverse, too. And having a Dyke March is pretty awesome. Still, it unsettles me, how easily Erin has moved on.

I turn away from Erin, shaking off the feeling and watching the people milling around. A short-haired blond girl in a T-shirt that says *This is what a bisexual looks like.* An indigenous group standing in a circle and drumming a steady beat. A girl my age, cute and topless and entirely covered in gold glitter so that she looks like a sparkly statue. A huge group of people on bicycles, rainbow flags waving, rainbow ribbons woven through wheels. One has a tiara-wearing dachshund in her bicycle basket. A group of drag kings. A couple pulling two adorable babies in a red wagon piled with toys and trailed by balloons.

I'm just staring and staring, trying to take it all in.

Then the Dykes on Bikes begin revving their engines, and the electricity in the air is so intense I can practically see the sparks all around us. I look at one of the women: an older dyke, very fat, with a black tank top and tattooed arms and a rainbow boa around her neck, and she looks right back at me and winks. I'm grinning so wide my face hurts.

"Come on." Erin grabs my arm. "We're marching with the university group, Jack's friends. Okay?"

I nod and follow, and we merge from the sidewalk into the march itself. The motorcycles are still revving, revving, and my heart is hammering, and then we're off.

I'm walking beside Erin, right behind Jack and Brooke and Kade and the others whose names I don't remember, and I feel, again, on the edge of tears. It's just so overwhelming being in a crowd like this, of women and trans people and allies, feeling this level of support and acceptance. And then I notice that Jack and top-less-electrical-tape girl are holding out a huge banner in front of us. "What's the group?" I ask Erin. "Like, U of T Pride or something?"

Erin shakes their head, and an expression I can't read flickers across their face. "No, it's . . . um, it's a poly group."

I stop walking. "Wait, what? Did you join? Is that how you met Jack?"

"I met him at the coffee shop. But yeah, I went to one of their meetings last week." Erin takes my hand. "Come on, you can't stop here . . ."

Someone bumps into me from behind and I keep walking, glancing over my shoulder to see a tall person with spiky hair and a rainbow-painted sign: *Polyamorous and Proud.*

Just fucking great. "You joined a poly group and you didn't even tell me?"

"Because I knew you'd be like this," Erin says, sighing. Like I'm the one who's being an asshole.

"I told you, though. I told you I can't be with you if you're seeing other people."

"And I told you I can't be with you if that means I can never be with anyone else."

I feel like they just slapped me. I pull my hand away and push my way through the people, out of the march and onto the sidewalk.

Erin follows, obviously pissed off. "You're overreacting, Talia. I went to one meeting, okay? It's not like I'm even seeing anyone. Why are you making this a huge deal?"

"Overreacting? Are you serious?" I fold my arms across my chest, feeling as though I'm trying to hold myself together. "You join a poly group your first week in Toronto. You don't bother telling me about it, or about whatever's going on with you and Jack. Even though you know how I feel. You're texting me, all like, *oh yeah I really miss you come to Toronto we have to talk.* Like you want to fix things, like you want to make this work. Then, even though I totally said I can't do this if you're with other people, you act like we're still together. And now you expect me to march behind a fucking *Poly and Proud* banner? Jesus, Erin."

I'm so angry. I feel like I've been lied to. And I can't believe that everything just went from so awesome to total crap in a heartbeat.

"I did miss you," Erin says softly. "I did want to fix things."

"By lying to me? That's messed up." I'm fighting back tears, but they're tears of fury. "You didn't want to fix things enough to cancel your plans with your friends, or to march with me instead of them."

Erin's eyes are shining with tears, too. "I don't know how to explain. It's . . . being here . . . it's like, all of a sudden there are all these people that get what I've been going through, that I can talk to about stuff . . ."

"You could talk to me," I say.

"I know. But this is different. I was the ONLY nonbinary person at our school, Talia. That was . . . it was hard. And no one really understood. So coming here, it was like . . . another world. One where I actually fit."

It stings, this idea that I wasn't enough. That even though I told Erin everything, there were things they didn't share. "But you didn't join a nonbinary group," I say. "You joined a poly group. And I don't have a problem with you talking to people. I just don't want you dating them. Is that so hard to understand?"

Erin nods. "I've been up front about it, though. I've said I want a more open relationship. I've been saying that for ages. You just don't listen."

"I do listen! And I've said I don't want that. That you have to pick. And I thought—I thought you were picking me. But I guess you were just lying."

"I never lied to you," Erin says, almost shouting; loud enough that people turn and stare.

"Not directly, maybe," I say, and I start to cry. Erin's never shouted at me, not in the whole time we've known each other, and I feel like we're turning into other people: ugly, jealous, shouting people. "But not telling me stuff? That's a kind of lying."

"Talia. Stop. What haven't I told you?"

"About Jack, for one thing."

"He's a friend, Talia. That's all. Yeah, I like him. But nothing has happened between us. You think I should text you every time I make a new friend? Or every time I feel slightly attracted to someone?"

"No, of course not. But . . ."

"Look, we broke up, right? Before I left Victoria?"

Did we? "I guess," I say. "But then we sort of got back together . . ."

"Well. We slept together," Erin says. "I'm not sure that's the same thing. I mean—it doesn't change anything, does it?"

Doesn't it? I swallow and my throat feels like there's a knife lodged in it. "I don't know." I feel like I don't know anything anymore.

"I didn't want to break up," Erin says. "I really, really didn't."

"Then why do we have to?" I'm crying now.

"Talia. I can't keep doing this." Erin runs a hand through their hair, leaving it messed up and spiky. "God, we just go round in the same circles."

"I just don't get it," I say. "Why isn't this . . . you and me . . . enough for you?"

"Because—and you would know this if you ever even tried to listen—It. Isn't. What. I. Want." Erin's voice is hard-edged, as spiky as their hair, but their eyes are shining with tears. "And you know what, Talia? I am so, so sick of you acting like everything is about you. Like you're the better person, the more loyal person. Like you're the one who is always in the right. Like wanting to be monogamous somehow makes you superior. Like poly relationships aren't just as real and valid. I mean, we want different things, okay, fine—it sucks, but neither of us can help that. But you act like everything is my fault."

"I never said that," I protest.

"Maybe not in so many words. But don't you think that? Honestly?"

I don't say anything for a moment. Erin's the one who changed, I think. Erin's the one who started wanting something different. Doesn't that kind of make it their fault?

"Wanting to see other people doesn't change how I feel about you," Erin says. "It doesn't mean that I'm not terrified of losing my best friend."

I start to cry. And then a hand lands on my shoulder. "Talia? Are you okay?"

I turn.

It's Mark.

CHAPTER TWENTY-ONE

MARK

I wake up in the morning, and when I open my eyes, it takes a moment for me to remember where I am: on a couch in the basement at Derek and Kenny's house. I stretch out, smiling as I remember Jeremy and me sneaking back inside last night, long after everyone else was asleep.

In the end, we hadn't been able to find a cab, so we walked almost an hour back to Greektown. I didn't mind. It felt good to be stretching my legs, soaking up as much of the downtown experience as I could. Besides, after our chaotic arrival in the city, and our hectic trip into the Village, the walk home was my first real opportunity to get to know Jeremy.

He's really smart. Like, straight honors and full scholarship smart, but in a way that goes beyond just being good at school. He's the kind of person who's interested in all kinds of things, and he knows a lot about every one of them. We talked the whole way back to Greektown—about books, politics, sports, travel, you name it.

I realized at some point that he was doing most of the talking, but I didn't feel left out of the conversation. In fact, it was kind of the opposite, as if the usual pressure to contribute my own words and observations had disappeared, and someone else was doing the heavy lifting for a change.

I can take up a lot of space, and it was kind of nice to listen to someone else who has the same kind of confidence that I have. Someone who, if I'm being honest, isn't as shallow as I am.

I don't mean that in a self-deprecating way. It's more like Jeremy made me interested in stuff that I don't really think about. He made me want to be more *interesting,* to read more, think about stuff beyond just parties and sports and boys.

Back at Derek and Kenny's place, he'd pulled out a key, and we slipped inside.

"Do you think your uncles would miss a beer or two?" I ask him.

"Probably not," he laughs. "Go for it. They should be in the fridge."

"You want to join me?"

"No, I'm cool. I don't drink."

He'd said it casually, as if it didn't matter, and I realized that of course it doesn't. I decided to follow his lead and have a mineral water.

We went into the backyard and sat for a while, chatting. Then we just lay back in some recliners, staring quietly up at the stars. When Jeremy stood, I thought maybe something was going to happen, but he just showed me to the extra room in the basement. Before I even had a chance to make a move, he smiled and wished me good night, and he slipped back upstairs.

I sit up now and reach over to turn on a lamp, then look around and get my first good look at the room I've crashed in. It's wallpapered, an elaborate deep red pattern, and there are framed vintage movie posters all over the walls, broken only by a huge-screen TV on one end, and a tall antique cabinet, shelves full of DVDs behind glass doors. I'd kill for a TV room like this.

As I reach down to shrug into my shorts, I hear tiny footsteps approaching down the hallway. A tiny, gray-haired terrier appears in the doorway and stops, staring at me.

"Hello, pooch," I say. "Where are all the people?"

It cocks its head and lets out a tiny, dignified bark, then turns and disappears back down the hallway. I pull on my T-shirt and follow it, becoming aware for the first time of the smell of something delicious cooking somewhere in the house.

Upstairs I find a powder room, where I pee and wash my face, and then I follow my nose toward the smell of breakfast. In the kitchen, I find Derek standing at the stove and Babs sitting across the island from him, sipping a coffee and chatting.

"Well, hello there," says Derek. "I see you've met Toto."

"He led me back to society," I say, bending to scratch the dog under the chin.

"Jeremy tells us that you were relieved of your family duties," says Babs.

"More like escaped," I say. "My mom is probably figuring out how to legally disown me, right about now."

"I'm sure you'll make it up to her," she says with a wink.

"Where's Shirley?" I ask.

"She's helping Kenny with a project," she says. She exchanges a grin with Derek, but they don't explain further.

"You hungry?" asks Derek.

"Always."

He slides a breakfast sandwich onto a plate and hands it to me. "Coffee's on the buffet," he says, pointing. "Jeremy's in the backyard. He just got back from a run."

I carry my coffee and sandwich into the backyard, where I find Jeremy doing some yoga stretches on the grass.

"You put me to shame," I say through a mouthful of breakfast sandwich. I hold it up to him. "You've earned one of these, that's for sure."

He smiles. "I already grabbed some oatmeal. I'm vegan. You sleep all right?"

"Like a baby."

"Great. I'm going to catch a shower, then I was thinking we could make our way downtown. Meet up with the crew for the Dyke March. I could probably rustle up a fresh T-shirt and some shorts if you want."

"That'd be awesome," I say.

After he's gone inside, I decide to rip off the Band-Aid, so I pull out my phone and call my mother.

"Mark," she answers. Her voice is unreadable, like an oracle's.

"On a scale of one to ten, how much trouble am I in?" I ask.

"How does fifty suit you?" she asks.

"I'll make it up to you," I say. "Promise. How's Grandma?"

She sighs. "She's okay. The doctor thinks she can be discharged tomorrow. I hate the thought of sending her back to that condo all by herself. There are some uncomfortable decisions ahead of us."

"Are you and Gary getting along?"

"Quit changing the subject, Mark." I can tell by her crisp tone that the answer is no. "We're under enough pressure here without you and Talia taking off into the city like this. To be honest, I'm more surprised by your cousin's behavior than I am by yours."

"Gee, thanks," I say.

"Do I need to remind you of your drunken frolic from last week? Is Talia with you, at least?"

"No," I say. "She's with Erin. Her partner. I guess."

"Well, she's only barely responded to her father's texts, and he's almost as pissed off as I am."

"Maybe it's good for her," I say. "To be out on her own. Standing up for herself."

"Well, I'm certainly not going to bring that theory up to him. Are you coming to the hospital today?"

I cringe. "I don't think I'll make it today."

"Great," she says.

"Mom, I'm sorry. Really. I'll be there tomorrow, I promise. But today . . . there's just . . . somebody. Somebody I'm trying to get to know."

She is silent for a moment. "You're staying somewhere safe?"

"Yes," I say quickly. "Very safe. I promise. There are positive adult role models everywhere."

She sighs. "Tomorrow, Mark. I want you here to see your grandmother tomorrow."

"I promise," I tell her. "Seriously. I love you."

"I love you, too," she says.

"Thanks, Mom. You really are the best."

"You realize that I'm immune to your charm routine, right? I'm your mother. I'm used to your tricks. I'll see you tomorrow."

———

"There's a Dyke March in Halifax, too," I say to Jeremy, leaning into his ear and speaking really loudly over the roar of the motorcyclists. "But it's kind of small."

"This one's only been around for about twenty years," says Jeremy. "It was super controversial at the start. They didn't have trans inclusion until a few years later, and a lot of people still complain about it not being inclusive enough, because cis men aren't invited. Personally, I think it's pretty rad."

"Inclusive my ass," Betty yells over the noise of the crowd. "Women and people of color and the trans community have always been part of the movement, but until we carved out space for ourselves, we were always playing second fiddle to gay men. Typical patriarchal bullshit. Cis men dominate pretty much every other forum; they'll survive not being included in this one."

Miraculously, we've managed to connect with Dax and Betty despite the crowds. The four of us are crammed together at the edge of the sidewalk, near the starting point. The Dykes on Bikes roar past us, signaling the beginning of the march.

"Awesome!" I yell. "I love parades!"

Betty pokes me in the arm. "It's not a parade, it's a march! At least try to get that much straight, pardon the expression."

I give her a thumbs-up. "Got it."

I keep trying to steal glances at Jeremy without being too obvious. It's hard to get a good read on him. Some moments, I feel like he's into me. Others, I feel like he's just a good guy showing a newbie around the city.

"Thanks for letting me hang out!" I say, leaning over to speak directly into his ear. "I would have been kind of overwhelmed if I were here by myself!"

"Hey, no problem," he says. "I have to admit, it's kind of selfish of me! I'm hoping you can return the favor!"

"What do you mean?"

"I'm going to be moving to Halifax in about a month. I've been accepted into Dalhousie for pre-med!"

I turn to look at him, my mouth hanging open.

"That's awesome!" I say.

"We'll have some time to get to know each other," he says.

I'm just starting to register how completely thrilled this news makes me, and what that might mean, when I turn and notice two people having an argument, just a few feet away from me. One of them turns away from the other, and I realize with surprise that it's Talia. She looks really upset.

I turn back to Jeremy. "That's my cousin!" I say. "I have to go see if she's all right. Don't leave this spot!"

I press my way through the crowd, coming up behind Talia and reaching out to put my hand on her shoulder.

"Talia, are you okay?"

She turns to look at me. "Mark," she says. She opens her mouth to say more, but she can only shake her head. She looks like she is on the verge of tears.

"What did you do to her?" I ask the person standing behind her.

"It's fine, Mark," says Talia. "They didn't do anything."

"Are you Erin?" I ask.

"Yeah," says Erin, who looks really uncomfortable, and I wonder what, exactly, I'm walking in on.

"Talia," I ask again, "is everything okay?"

"Yeah," she says. Then, "No. I don't know." She looks even more upset, like she's about to cry, and impulsively I lean in and give her a hug. She freezes for a moment, then presses into me, and I can feel her crying against my chest.

"Jesus Christ," I say to Erin. "What the fuck? What happened?"

"Mark," says Talia, pulling away, wiping at her eyes with the back of her hand. "It's fine."

"It's not fine," I say. "You're obviously not fine. Listen, I don't want to pressure you at all, but do you want to come with me? I'm here with some friends."

She looks back at Erin. They just shake their head, as if they don't know what to say.

"Yes," says Talia after a moment. "Please. Let's go."

"Talia," says Erin, reaching out and touching her on the arm.

"I just need to be away from you right now, Erin," says Talia. She turns back to me. "Can we please just go?"

CHAPTER TWENTY-TWO
TALIA

I follow Mark, pushing through the crowds. I glance back over my shoulder once, but Erin is gone—probably back with Jack and the others already. Mark takes my arm and pulls me to a clear patch of sidewalk.

"Are you okay? What happened?" he asks.

I shake my head. "We . . . had a fight, I guess."

"No shit. That much I figured out by myself."

My laugh comes out more like a sob. "Erin wants a"—I make air quotes—"more open relationship."

"As in, Erin's met someone else?"

"Yeah, basically." Then I shake my head, feeling stupidly protective still. "They're not cheating or anything. This is a conversation that we've been having for a while." I cross my arms in front of me. "Okay, tell me something: why do I feel so freaking ridiculous and uncool for wanting to be monogamous?"

Mark shifts from one foot to the other, looking uncomfortable. "Uh. You shouldn't."

"The thing is, even if Erin agreed not to see other people, it'd just be because of what *I* want. Not what *they* want. It's been two weeks and Erin's like a different person already. Erin loves Toronto. They've made all these new friends; they're super happy. I'm like this stupid weight that's just holding them back." I swallow painfully. "I don't want to be that person."

"So . . . it's over?"

"Yeah. It's over." I don't want to start crying again. "I feel like I should be happy for them, you know? That they've met all these people and . . . I mean, I know how hard it was for them, at school." We were good together, though. I know we were. We had fun. It wasn't *all* hard.

"Seriously? *Happy* for them?" Mark's eyebrows shoot up, and the corners of his mouth twitch like he's holding back a laugh. "You are way, WAY too hard on yourself, Talia. You just broke up. You're allowed to be pissed off. You're supposed to think your ex is an asshole, right? It's right there in the rulebook. Or it would be, if there were one."

I chew on my bottom lip. "I guess." I don't want to be like that: angry and self-righteous. When you've loved someone for so long, you don't stop caring about them when things change. When you realize you want different things. So I want to be happy for Erin . . . but I think it'll take me some time to get there. "Anyway," I say, needing to change the subject, "what are you doing here? Watching the March? Where's Paige?"

He nods. "With my mom. Long story. Well—not that long, really, but let's just say I'm going to be grounded for the rest of my life." He grins. "So we should make the most of this weekend! Are you up for meeting a few people?"

"Um. Yeah? Sure."

———

Turns out Mark's not only made some friends—a tall, thin guy called Dax and a cute girl with white-blond hair and bright red lipstick, whose name is Betty—he's also developed a massive, can't-even-talk-to-him-without-blushing crush on a very good-looking guy named Jeremy. Not bad for being in the city for, what, fourteen hours?

We all watch the Dyke March together. I feel like I'm in some kind of weird dream: everything that's happened in the last few days—the funeral, meeting Paige and Mark, all the weirdness with our parents, Grandma, the cottage, Mariana and Darren and Shirley and Babs and Erin and Jack and the epic, roaring, sparkling rainbow of queerness swirling around us right now . . . I shake my head, close my eyes, and open them again. A topless girl on a bicycle waves and tosses me something: a candy, and a square of paper advertising a queer dance party. I stick the paper in my pocket and the candy in my mouth and savor the burst of strawberry-flavored sweetness.

Despite the craziness of it all, despite knowing how mad my dad is going to be, despite what happened with Erin, I feel kind of okay. The marchers—with their waves, their signs, their chants, their smiles—are lifting me up. Even standing here, watching, I am a part of it all.

The world feels like a much bigger place than it did a week ago.

Too soon, the march ends, and people start to drift away. "Now what?" Betty asks. "Shall we move this party to a new locale?"

I shake my head. "I think I'm going to head to the condo," I say. "Get it over with."

"Don't do that," Mark says. "Come on. Let's go get something to eat—I'm starving—and decide where to go tonight." He does a little shimmy. "We've got to go dancing!"

I make a face. "I'm not in a dancing mood."

He puts his hands together, like he's begging or praying or something. "Come on, Talia. It's Pride weekend! We're in Toronto!"

"I just ended a three-year relationship, Mark."

"I know. And . . . I'm really sorry." He hesitates, then goes on. "But getting yelled at by your dad isn't going to make you

196

feel any better," he says. "And once you turn yourself in, no way he'll let you go out again."

Which is undeniably true.

Dax and Betty and Jeremy are tactfully pretending not to listen. Betty reapplies her lipstick, using her smartphone as a mirror. Jeremy is reading a flyer. Dax is staring into space.

"I just . . ." I trail off. Erin's probably out having fun with their friends. And Mark's right: Dad's not going to be happy with me. Sitting around at the condo, with him and Janet mad at me—and probably still being all weird with each other—is not going to make for a fun evening. "Fine," I say. "Food. Dancing. Let's go have some fun."

"YES!" Mark says, and he looks so genuinely happy that I can't help grinning back at him. Dax, Betty, and Jeremy abandon their pretense of not listening and all start cheering: "Woot. Woot. Woot!" It's totally goofy but it makes me laugh.

Maybe tonight will be okay after all.

———

Every restaurant in the Village itself is packed and lined up onto the sidewalk, so we walk toward Carlton in search of a sushi place that Dax says is good and cheap.

Betty falls into pace beside me. "Didn't mean to eavesdrop, but I gathered that you just had a breakup," she says. "I'm sorry. That sucks."

"Yeah. Erin and I were together since grade ten, you know? So it's hard . . ." And I find myself telling her all about it, which is weird because I am usually a pretty private person. She's a good listener, though, and somehow the fact that she doesn't know me or Erin makes her easy to talk to.

"Wow," she says when I finally wind down. "That's a lot to sort through. But I guess it opens up some possibilities, right?"

"You mean like dating other people?" I wrinkle my nose. "The last thing I want to do is get involved with someone else."

Betty shakes her head. "No. I mean, yeah, sure. That too. But I meant . . . when you're with someone for a long time, you kind of define yourself in relation to them, right? Especially being together all through high school. I had the same boyfriend from when I was fourteen to eighteen, and I thought we'd be together forever. Get married, make babies, happy-ever-after. I was totally crushed when we split up, but now—that was a couple years ago—I am so glad we did. Because I'm a different person, you know? Got into photography, made new friends, met Parul . . ."

Erin-and-Talia, I think. "Yeah," I say. "We had all these plans. We were going to live together, take the same classes at university in Victoria. And then they decided to go to U of T, and I couldn't afford it, and then they left early because of this job, and now . . ." I shrug. "I thought I knew what the next few years would look like, and now I have no clue. I mean, I have no idea who I even am without Erin."

"Which is hard, right?" Betty nods. "But also kind of cool, because now you get to decide that for yourself."

She's right. It's a slightly dizzying thought.

There's still this black cloud hanging over me, still a heavy ache in my chest. Sadness. Anger. Missing Erin and wishing things were different. But that cloud is shot through with a silvery streak that feels like . . . I don't know exactly.

Anticipation, maybe?

Like the sun's going to come out again.

Like I'm heading off on a road trip with no particular destination, just the open road stretching out ahead.

CHAPTER TWENTY-THREE

MARK

The sushi is pretty good, but not as good as back home. Secretly, I'm kind of happy to have finally found something that Halifax does better than Toronto. As much as I'm having a great time, and Pride is crazy fun and exciting, like an endlessly sprawling party, I find myself with a new appreciation of the old home-town. Toronto is hot as hell, sticky, and close, without the fresh smell of the ocean, and the tide clearing out the air twice a day. Halifax is also missing the sprawl, and definitely the anonym-ity. At home, you can't walk for a block without running into one or twenty people you've known your whole life. Sure, that can get a bit annoying, but staring at the giant crowds of people, I can see how the alternative I've grown up with is actually kind of cool. Comforting.

Don't get me wrong, though—so far, this is one of the best weekends of my life. If it weren't for Jeremy, and the game-changing information that he'll be living in Halifax in, like, a month, I'd already be planning how to move here after graduation. Now . . . it's way too early to know, obviously, but still—there's something about meeting him that feels . . . right.

Betty gets a text and her face gets kind of goofy and lovesick.

"Parul got off work early," she says. "She's going to come meet us. Where should I tell her?"

"Are we going to dance?" I ask.

"Oh, we're going to dance," says Jeremy. "Only question is where."

"What are the options?" I ask.

Jeremy and Betty both look at Dax, who's been distracted and very quiet, just picking at his food.

"Come on, Dax," says Betty. "You're the expert."

Dax sighs. "Well, it depends. If we want to get into a club, we'll have to go while it's still early, before there are bouncers on duty. It might not work, but it's the only way we'll get in with minors. Even if that works, we'll be stuck in the same place all night."

"Let's just wander," says Betty. "Maybe we can find some all-age shows."

"That sounds perfect," I say. "I want to check out as much as I can before I turn back into a pumpkin."

"Me too," says Talia. "Sounds great."

"Whatever," says Dax. "It doesn't matter."

"What is wrong with you?" asks Betty.

"You haven't heard from Clem?" asks Jeremy.

Dax shakes his head. "He texted me this morning and said he'd meet us at the march, and I haven't heard from him since. I guess I should stop getting my hopes up."

"Honestly," says Betty, shaking her head, annoyed. "I don't understand why you keep letting that guy string you along."

I'm kind of surprised to hear this. It seemed to me when I saw them last night that Dax is at least a couple of years older than Clem, and he seemed to be kind of in charge, helping Clem out, making sure he got home okay.

"You know how much I like him," he says.

"Yeah, we know sweetie," says Betty, "but he's been dicking you around like this all summer. To hell with him. Don't wait around for someone who isn't going to give you the respect that you show them."

I find myself thinking of Jareth, back in Halifax, waiting to hear from me. I don't need to ask myself if I've been leading him on, the way Clem has been to Dax. I have been, no question. The thing about Jareth is that he's really sweet, and a great friend, but as much as I hate to admit it, he's always been more into me than I am into him. Jareth was a convenient and available first boyfriend, and I realize now that I've always been waiting for something better to come along. Darren, which obviously didn't work out. Jeremy, who might be a different story.

"Come on," says Jeremy, putting his arm around Dax's shoulder and starting to drag him out of the booth. "We need to get you on your feet."

Dax looks like he's trying his best to stay annoyed and upset, but then something in his face relaxes and he laughs. "Okay, fine, I admit it. I need some dance therapy."

———————

Back on the street, Betty texts briefly with Parul and then turns and begins marching in a specific direction. "She's going to meet us at the disco stage," she says.

"I love disco," I say.

"Ugh," Talia whispers to me with a bit of a smirk. "I hate it."

"It's just one dish on the smorgasbord," I say.

She laughs. "Don't worry, I can pretend."

In front of us, Betty is walking quickly, obviously excited to get to Parul, and Jeremy has his arm draped over Dax's shoulder. From the bits and pieces of their conversation that float back at me, I can tell that he's giving Dax a pep talk, trying to cheer him up.

"Jeremy seems like a great guy," says Talia.

"He really is," I say. After a moment, I tell her, "He's going to Dalhousie in the fall. He's going to be moving to Halifax."

"No way!" she says, turning to look at me with a big smile.

"Yeah," I say. "My mission over the next few hours is to make him fall in love with me."

She laughs. "Thanks for persuading me to hang out with you guys," she says. "I'm glad that I get to experience Pride, even without Erin. It all feels so happy and positive and . . . and safe."

"Do you feel unsafe in Victoria?" I ask, surprised.

"No," she says. "Victoria's great. I just mean in the broader perspective, you know? Things are good back home, but I feel like something's happened over the last couple of years. I don't know if it's the rise of Trump, or the fact that there are a million trolls out there doing everything they can to make people feel like shit, but I've been reminded lately that there's still a lot of work to be done. The hate that's out there toward queer people doesn't exist in a vacuum."

"Yeah," I say. I hate to admit how little attention I pay to politics, but it's hard not to feel uneasy lately. Even in Halifax, I've heard stories recently about people getting beaten up outside gay bars.

"Here, though," she says, gesturing broadly to indicate everything around us, "it's a whole different universe—a reminder that we're everywhere, and we're awesome, and we support one another. I guess that's what I mean by safe. Not safe in the moment, but safe in the world."

"I'm sorry about you and Erin," I say.

She looks at me and smiles. It's a bit sad, but it's a smile. "It'll be okay," she says. "I'll be okay."

There's a lightness to the way Talia is moving and talking and acting that I haven't seen before. I think she's right. She will be okay.

We turn a corner and I can hear disco pounding down the street. I know it's totally cheesy, but I really do love disco. It's happy and propulsive and fabulously retro, and now I can't wait to start dancing.

Ahead of us, Betty breaks into a little run and then I see Parul standing on the sidewalk, waiting for her. They collide into an embrace, and then a lingering, full-on kiss. When they pull apart and turn back to us, waiting for us to catch up, they both have huge smiles on their faces.

I realize that I want what they have. Something honest and kind and loving. A relationship in which two people look at each other as if they want nothing else than to be together.

"For the love of Gaga," says Dax as we approach. "Do you think you could tamp it down just a little bit? I don't want to be reminded of true love right now."

"You picked the wrong weekend for that, Dax," says Parul as she reaches up to kiss him on the cheek.

The next few hours are a blur of laughter and music and dancing. It seems like every venue we move on to is bigger and better and more fun than the previous one. We're sweating and spinning, and by the time it starts to get dark, I'm completely exhausted.

"I have never danced this much in my life," I say to Jeremy as I stop and collapse, breathless, against a light post.

"I'm glad you're having a good time," he says. "I hope you're willing to return the favor and show me around Halifax this fall."

"Are you kidding?" I ask. "Of course. Although I'm not sure you're going to want to hang out with a high school boy when you've moved on to bigger and better things."

He laughs. "You're what, a year younger than me, tops? I think we can manage. I'm not into the bar scene, we'll keep things PG."

"Not *too* PG, I hope," I say, smiling.

His hand reaches down and grabs mine, and he shifts around so that he's facing me. We're almost exactly the same height, so we're able to look right into each other's eyes. He smiles, then closes his eyes and leans forward, and I realize that he's about to kiss me.

"Hang on," I blurt out before I know what I'm saying.

He pulls back, surprised. "Is everything okay?"

"Yes," I say quickly. "Everything's great. More than great. I really, really like you, and I really, really, *really* want to kiss you right now . . ."

"But?" he asks with a slight smile.

"There's a guy," I say. "Back home."

His smile fades. "You have a boyfriend."

"No," I say. "Well, yes. But it's been on the rocks for a while."

I can see the skepticism in his eyes. He drops my hand and steps back. "It's totally cool," he says, but there's a slight chill in his voice. "Seriously."

"No, wait," I say. I reach out and grab his hand again. He doesn't pull it away, but it's a loose grip. "I'm serious. I've been dating this guy for a while now, and I knew it was over before I left on this trip. I've known for a long time, actually. I was just too, I don't know, chickenshit, or self-absorbed, or whatever, to actually tell him it was over."

Jeremy just watches me, but his hand doesn't leave mine.

"I really am going to break it off with him," I say. "Like, as soon as I can. But I don't feel right making out with someone else before I do that. I know I'm probably being a total idiot, and I'm missing out on something really good here, but I just think it's the right thing to do."

He smiles again and squeezes my hand. "I think it's absolutely the right thing to do," he says. "You only get one chance to have a first kiss. You want the circumstances to be perfect."

"Yeah," I say, relieved. "Exactly. So, can I get a rain check on that first kiss?"

He pulls his hand away and leans in to give me a hug. "Absolutely. I'm not letting you off the hook that easy."

We push our way back into the fray, locating the rest of the gang. They're jumping up and down, singing along to "Dancing Queen," and they look like they're having the time of their lives. Talia, beaming, turns to wave at me as we approach. I squeeze over next to her.

"I think I'm ready to go back and face the music," I say. I have to yell into her ear for her to hear me.

She stops jumping and looks at me, surprised. "What about you and Jeremy?" she yells back.

"I'll explain later. Will you hate me if we leave now?"

"No!" she says. "Not at all! I mean, this has been amazing, but I'm exhausted."

We make our goodbyes, arranging to text before the parade the next day, and then we pull away from the dancers and begin the journey back to the condo. To reality.

CHAPTER TWENTY-FOUR

TALIA

It's past midnight when we get back to the condo, but Dad buzzes us in and opens the door. He does not look happy, to say the least. He waves us in, with a finger to his lips. "Janet and Paige are asleep," he says. "I suggest you two go to bed and we'll discuss this in the morning." He leans closer to me and sniffs. "Have you been drinking?"

"No." I frown. "I don't drink, you know that."

"You don't usually run away either," he says.

"I didn't run away," I protest.

"Shhh. We'll discuss it in the morning." He points to the hallway. "Mark, we're both in the spare room at the end of the hall. Talia, you can have the couch." He stomps off down the hall, every muscle radiating annoyance. Mark gives me a shrug and a rueful grin, and then follows him.

Well. Tomorrow morning's going to be fun.

I head to the bathroom to pee and brush my teeth, and then I swear under my breath as I realize I've left my bag—toothbrush, PJs, change of clothes—at Erin's place.

Crap. I guess I'll have to see them once more before this weekend is over.

———

I wake up the next morning to Paige bouncing on my feet. "Wake up!" she says. "You and Mark are in so much trouble."

I groan and sit up. I think the couch springs have left permanent imprints in my back and shoulders. "I know," I say, getting to my feet and stretching. I feel surprisingly lighthearted, though.

Mark shuffles out of the kitchen holding two mugs of coffee and hands one to me. "Your dad's getting dressed. Mom's just out of the shower. You ready for the inquisition?"

I take the mug and sit back down on the couch. "Ready as I'll ever be."

I don't usually drink coffee, but Mark's loaded it with cream and sugar, and it feels like exactly the right thing. Paige lies on the carpet, buried in a fantasy novel, and Mark and I sit side by side, sipping in silence while we wait.

All too soon, Janet and Dad emerge, showered and dressed and ready to give us hell. They perch on straight back chairs across the room.

Mark tries to get the first word in. "Mom, first of all, I'm really sorry about taking off when you came to pick me up. I know that was kind of obnoxious—"

"You shouldn't have been in Toronto in the first place," my dad says. "We left you at the cottage with an important job to do. And Paige to take care of, for that matter. Dragging a ten-year-old to the city was the most irresponsible—"

"Gary, if you don't mind?" Janet holds her hand up, palm toward him, in a not-very-subtle stop sign. "Mark was talking to me, I believe."

"I hope he was apologizing to us both," my dad says. "Talia has always been a very responsible girl. This whole thing is completely out of character for her. Talia, whose idea was it to come to Toronto?"

Jesus. They're still at each other's throats.

Mark jumps in before I have time to think up a reply. "It was my idea, Uncle Gary. I'm so sorry. It's just that I've always wanted to be in Toronto for Pride, and we were so close—"

"I wanted to see Erin," I say. "It was my choice to come, so don't blame Mark."

"There, you see?" Janet looks at my father. "Your perfect daughter wasn't exactly kidnapped by my son, so please stop trying to make out that this is all his fault."

Gary raises one eyebrow. "All I'm saying is that until this weekend, she'd—"

"STOP FIGHTING!" Paige shouts, and she bursts into tears.

Mark gives his mom a disgusted look and puts an arm around Paige. "Look, I'm sorry. Talia's sorry. We're both sorry. But whatever is going on between you guys—" He shrugs. "—It's not helping anything."

Janet and my dad exchange looks but say nothing. "I want to go see Grandma," Paige says between sobs.

"How is she?" I ask, feeling bad that I haven't already checked in.

"Not bad," Dad says. "Much better, actually."

"Good. Um. Can we go see her?" I give him a pleading look. "Please? I've been looking through all the stuff at the cottage, and there's all these old photos of her . . . I'd like to see her."

Janet sighs. "We probably should. We told her we'd be back this morning." She points a finger at Mark. "We are going to have some more conversations about this, you understand? This isn't over."

Mark nods, and I think he's trying to look glum, but he isn't really pulling it off. I bet he's thinking about Jeremy.

———

Grandma is sitting up in bed when we arrive, and other than the fact that she is wearing a hospital gown, she looks pretty good. She has a tray in front of her, filled with empty dishes, so I guess she's eating.

"Hi, Grandma," I say, bending to give her a hug. "How's the food?"

She pulls a face. "Don't ask. How's my cottage?"

"It's great," I tell her.

"I can't wait to get back up there," she says.

"Really?" I glance at my father. "Um, you're planning to keep it, then?"

Grandma pushes her tray away. "I told you all that was going to be a family decision, and I meant it." She looks at my father, and then at Janet. "But right now, it still belongs to me and I want to go there. Now."

There's an awkward pause while Janet and Dad look anywhere but at each other. Then Mark says, "Yeah, I'm in."

"Me too," I say quickly.

"I'll take you both for a ride in my Mustang," Grandma says.

Mark stares at her and a slow grin spreads across his face. "That's *your* Mustang? Not Grandpa's?"

"Hah!" I say. "Sexist assumptions, much?"

"Like you didn't assume the same," he says, and I just shake my head and laugh because he's totally right.

———

Janet and Dad slip out to talk to the doctors, and when we meet them downstairs at the coffee shop half an hour later, they're both frowning. "Well, we need to talk," Dad says.

"What?" I ask, feeling worried. Grandma seems okay, but they look so serious.

"Grandma's being discharged in a few days, so—"

"That's great," Mark says.

"It is," Janet says, "but she'll need some support at home, or perhaps even a different living situation. We need to discuss things with her and make arrangements." She rubs her face and I notice the dark circles under her eyes. Dad looks wrecked, too: I don't think either of them has had much sleep. And their father just died a few days ago, I tell myself, with a flicker of guilt. I feel bad about how little I've thought about him since the funeral. "Anyway," Dad says, "we're going to get you three onto flights as soon as we can— back to Halifax for Mark and Paige, back to Victoria for you, Talia. Janet and I will stay here and wrap things up, get Grandma settled. Talia, you should call your mother and give her a heads-up."

"What about the cottage?" Mark asks.

"That's not the highest priority right now," Janet says.

"We might as well finish up there, though," Mark says. "We have all kinds of stuff half-sorted, not put away properly . . . And Grandma's car is at a mechanic's shop halfway to Muskoka."

Janet rubs her face again. "I don't know."

"Mark's right," I say. "We need to get the car back. And if no one's going to be at the cottage again this summer, we need to winterize it before we leave. If we don't at least turn off the water, there'll be burst pipes as soon as it freezes."

"I don't know . . ." Dad hesitates, then shakes his head. "How would you even get back there?"

Mark grins. "I think I know who we can hitch a ride with . . . and I'm pretty sure I know where we can find them."

———————

Over the next fifteen minutes, I listen—in what I can only describe as awe—while Mark manages to convince our parents that (A) letting us go back to the cottage to tidy up and winterize is a good idea, and (B) we should all go to the Pride Parade together to find Babs and Shirley, because (C) they can't possibly let us drive off to Muskoka with strangers.

His negotiating skills are seriously impressive. By the end, Dad is nodding like this was all his brilliant idea in the first place, and Janet is wondering out loud what she should wear to the parade.

"You're fine as you are," I say. She's wearing a short denim skirt and a blue top with little white flowers.

She makes a face. "Bit boring, though. In Halifax, I marched with PFLAG last year and we all wore rainbow tie-dye."

"I've never actually been to Pride," Dad admits. He sounds slightly apologetic. It's not that he isn't supportive, though: I've never wanted him to come with me because I like going with Erin and the kids from school. And he's not the type to join a group.

"That's cool that you're in PFLAG," I say to Janet. "I love seeing them in the parade."

"Yeah," Mark agrees, and he starts chanting: "Gay or straight, our kids are great!" He nudges his mom. "Right? You guys were the cutest."

She pushes him away, laughing. "Stop that."

Paige is practically jumping up and down with excitement. "Now? Can we go now?"

Janet glances at her watch. "Yes. If we want to get down there for the start of the parade, we should get moving. Mark and Talia, you should bring your stuff in case you don't come back here."

Oh, right. My stuff. I pull out my phone and fire off a quick text to Erin: Heading to the Parade. Can you meet me? And bring my bag?

The little dots appear that show they're typing a reply. I wait for the knot to twist in my stomach, for the tightness in my chest to build. But nothing happens. I feel remarkably okay.

The last time I saw them, I was in tears and we were yelling at each other in the street.

I know it's over between us. Maybe we'll stay friends, I'm not sure yet. But Erin-and-Talia is history.

But it's *our* history. And our time together deserves a better ending than that.

CHAPTER TWENTY-FIVE

MARK

As everyone kicks into gear, hustling to get ready to leave for the parade, I step out onto the balcony. There's something I need to do, and I need to be alone to do it, although I'm not sure you can ever feel totally alone in a city the size of Toronto. Behind me, I can see my family through the sliding glass doors, hurrying around, tidying up, and throwing stuff into bags. Above us and below us in the building, on either side of Grandma's little condo, other families are living *their* lives: fights and romances, meals and jokes and hangovers, various forms of grief and boredom and celebration. A million more variations on the theme are spread out in front of me, the endless flow of people living in the city, their dreams and disappointments, combining in a giant swell of noise.

My own problem is just the tiniest of drops in this ocean, but I know I can't pretend it doesn't matter anymore.

I skim down my texts to Jareth. My face flushes with shame when I realize how many times he's texted me over the past couple of weeks, how infrequently and impersonally I've texted him back. Does he feel about me the way that Talia feels, or felt, about Erin? Worse, did I lead him on, let him think that I felt the same way?

I start to compose a text, my thumbs stumbling, unable to come up with the right words.

Jareth, I owe you an apology. I've been

I stop, trying to figure out how to explain what "I've been." I delete the text, and quickly, before I can change my mind, I press the phone icon. I hold it to my ear, waiting as it dials through.

He picks up on the third ring.

"Hey," he says. His voice is unreadable. Not angry or sad. Not happy to hear from me, either. Just kind of flat, waiting.

"Hey," I say. I realize how unprepared for this I am. My typically cheerful demeanor has deserted me. My heart is pounding, and my mouth has gone dry. He waits. Letting me do the work, which is only fair. "How's it going?" I ask finally, buying myself time.

"It's all right," he says. "How's Ontario?" This time I can hear a distinct chill in his voice. He's pissed.

"It's cool. Busy. My grandmother had kind of an incident. A health problem. We were just at the hospital to see her."

I realize as I'm saying it that I'm trying to open space for an excuse. I didn't go looking for one, but it just popped into my mouth. A reason for sympathy. An explanation for my silence. It works.

"Oh, shit," he says, his voice softening. "I'm so sorry to hear that, Mark. Are you okay?"

I grab the bridge of my nose and squeeze, frustrated. I don't deserve his sympathy.

"Yeah," I say. "I'm fine. She's fine. I mean, she'll be okay. I just . . . I don't . . ."

"What is it?" he asks, his voice kind and gentle, trying to help me out.

"Jareth," I say, the words coming out in a rush, "I haven't been fair to you. I think you're awesome, and the last few months have been fun, but I've been pretending, I think."

"Pretending?" The pissed off tone is back.

"Yeah," I say. "Kind of. Pretending that I wanted something serious when I didn't. Letting you like me more than I like you."

The words come out so wrong that I have to force myself not to throw my phone off the balcony. I hear a sharp intake of breath on the other end of the phone that turns into an almost disbelieving chuckle.

"You are such an asshole," he says, dragging out the words so that each one feels like a tiny punch in the gut. "Let me guess. You met some cute guy, and now you're going to string him along for a while."

"No," I say. "It's not—"

He cuts me off. "You didn't meet someone else?"

I don't answer.

"Yeah," he says. "That's what I thought. Don't worry, Mark, I'll get over it. You're hot and fun, but it gets exhausting spending so much time with someone who's so deeply in love with himself."

He hangs up.

I stare at my phone for a minute, then slide it back into my shorts and lean on the railing, staring out at the city. *You're wrong, Jareth,* I think. *I'm definitely not in love with myself at the moment.*

There's a knock on the glass door behind me; it slides open and Talia steps out onto the balcony with me.

"Everything okay?" she asks.

I turn to look at her, and I manage a tight smile. "Nothing a fabulous, giant parade can't fix."

She raises an eyebrow but doesn't press it. "Cool. Everyone's ready. Time to get going."

I text Jeremy as we make our way downtown.

Where are you guys? On my way dt with whole family.

He hits me back with a street address right away.

Text when you're outside. I'll come let you in.

It turns out that the law office where Derek works has a rooftop patio that looks right down onto Yonge Street, and they host a parade viewing party every year. When we get off the insanely crowded subway and up to the street, the crowd takes my breath away. There are so many people that I can hardly believe it. Mom has Paige by the arm in a death grip, and I worry about what will happen if we get split up. It takes forever to squeeze through the crowd, but we finally make it to our destination and stand pressed up against the locked glass door. I text Jeremy, and a moment later he comes down and lets us in.

He greets me and Talia with big hugs, and then we introduce him around. When he shakes my mom's hand, she shoots me a totally obvious wink. He pretends not to notice.

"Are you sure this is okay?" Gary asks as we follow him up the stairs.

"Oh, yeah," says Jeremy. "The more the merrier, seriously."

"He's cute," my mother whispers. It comes out louder in the stairwell than I think she intended.

"Right?" asks Talia. Paige giggles. I just roll my eyes at them.

The patio is awesome. There are a few dozen people, just two stories above street level, with a perfect view down onto the street. Shirley spots us when we arrive and runs over to give us all hugs, Mom and Gary included. She immediately starts chatting them up, and I can tell that they're going to have no problem letting us drive back with them.

Babs approaches. "Guess what, bud? I got in touch with my old buddy Jacques, who owns a custom shop in Vaughan.

221

Turns out he's got the right part for the Mustang. Should be an easy fix."

"That's awesome," I say.

Shirley sticks her head over. "Your mom here tells me you kids need a ride back toward cottage country. You think you can be ready to roll once the parade is over?"

"Yeah," I say. "For sure."

"Great," says Babs. "We'll just have to stop back at Kenny and Derek's to pick up the truck."

"Here it comes!" someone yells.

Everyone moves to the railing, squeezing to find space to watch as the parade approaches. Jeremy slides up next to me, and I look at him and grin.

"Pretty great, isn't it?" he asks.

"It's like a fairytale," I say.

Below us, an enormous pride flag, stretched out to the length of a city block, is being carried along the street. People are singing and dancing, and music is pumping through the streets, a chaotic mix of Latin and dance and even the brassy strains of a marching band. I can see them a bit farther back along the street, looking like they came straight off a football field.

"It's hard not to feel good about yourself in a scene like this," says Jeremy. He shoots me a big, beautiful grin.

I smile at him, and he reaches out and squeezes my shoulder. "You okay?" he asks.

"Yeah!" I say, trying to muster up some genuine enthusiasm. "This is amazing."

"But?" he asks.

"I don't want to be a buzzkill," I say.

He puts his arm around my neck and whispers into my ear, "You couldn't be a buzzkill if you tried."

"I called Jareth," I say. "The guy I told you about last night. I told him that it was over. He—he wasn't overly impressed."

"Oh, that sucks," he says. "Breaking up is never easy, but it was the right thing to do. You should be proud of yourself."

"I don't feel very proud of myself," I say.

"Hey," he says, "that's blasphemy. It's Pride."

I look at him and smile, and before I know what's happening, he's pressing toward me and we're kissing. Maybe it should be weird, totally out in the open like this, with all these people around, my mother and sister just a few feet away, but it doesn't feel weird. It feels perfect, as if everyone and everything has melted into one perfect cluster of noise and happiness and, well, pride.

He pulls away and reaches up to touch my cheek with the back of his hand. "Feel better?" he asks.

"Yeah," I say, leaning up into his face to give him another quick kiss. "I feel great."

"There she is!" yells Shirley, and the crowd on the balcony begins to cheer extra loud. I turn and look down to where she's pointing. Below us, a giant, glittering float is rolling past us. About a dozen shirtless guys are dancing around on the bed of the float, and in the middle, on a dazzling, sparkling dais, someone is singing into a giant microphone. She's in a long silver gown and has a giant bouffant of cotton candy hair piled on her head, topped with a tiara.

I realize that she's not actually singing, she's lip-syncing to ABBA. It's so perfectly done, though, with perfectly choreographed movements that have obviously been well rehearsed with the dancers. It takes me a moment to put it all together.

"Is that Kenny?" I ask Jeremy.

He turns to look at me. "Not right now," he says. "Right now, she's Candy Chiffon."

Candy Chiffon turns toward the balcony and takes a bow for us, and we all go wild.

The city might be a giant swell of noise, but right now it's come together in the perfect way.

After the parade has passed, we trickle back down onto the street, which feels kind of sad and empty, even though there are still tons of people milling about.

"We'll be back to the cottage sometime over the next few days," Mom says. "Try to keep things drama free until then."

"I promise," I say. I turn to Talia. "You ready to get back to the lake?"

She nods. "Yeah. But there's something I need to do first."

CHAPTER TWENTY-SIX

TALIA

It takes me longer than I expect to walk to Erin's brother's apartment building, just a block off Church Street. The parade may be over, but the Village streets are still packed with people celebrating Pride, vendors selling T-shirts and jewelry, volunteers handing out stickers: *Lesbian Pride! Ace Pride! Bi Pride!* I grab a *Queer Pride* one and stick it on my bare arm.

Erin's already outside, sitting on a stone wall by the entrance, when I arrive. My stomach tightens a little: I want to say something, and I'm worried I won't do it well enough. The last thing I want is another argument.

Erin stands up and holds out my bag.

I take it. "Thanks."

"Look, Talia—" Erin says at the exact moment that I say, "Um, Erin?"

We both laugh, and it's awkward but better.

"I wanted to say sorry," I say.

Erin's eyes widen. "I was going to say the same thing. I wasn't being fair."

"Maybe. But I accused you of lying, and you didn't do that. You never did that." I make a face. "You were honest. I just didn't like what you were saying."

"I could've been more clear," Erin says. "I should've ended it, I guess, if I wanted to move on. I just didn't want to lose you. We've been together for so long, you know? And . . . well, you're my best friend."

I blink back tears and notice that Erin is doing the same. "I hope we'll still be friends," I say. "But . . . not right away, okay? I think I need to not talk to you for a while. Not because I'm mad or anything. Just . . ."

Erin nods and swipes the back of their hand across their eyes. They've always hated to cry in front of anyone. Even me. "Yeah. I get it."

"I think . . . I think I kind of need to figure out who I am without you, if that makes sense." I swallow. "I guess that sounds like a big cliché."

"No. It doesn't. I mean, coming to Toronto . . . I feel like I've kind of been doing that. Figuring out who I am, on my own. I'm still doing it. And it's been exciting. But I think maybe it's easier to do it in a new place." Erin hesitates. "I don't think I could've done it without actually leaving Victoria."

"I might leave, too," I say. "Or I might not. I actually love the West Coast, so maybe I'll stay. I might think about Vancouver. If I did a co-op program, I could earn some money and go to school . . ." I'm suddenly not even sure I want to go to school: I've just assumed that that was what came next.

I'm not sure about anything at all.

"I'm going to miss you," Erin blurts out. "So much, Talia. More than you realize."

"I want you to be okay," I say. "I mean, better than okay. I want you to be happy."

"I know." Erin's voice wobbles. "I want you to be happy, too. And I'll always love you, you know. And whenever you're ready to be friends . . . well, no pressure or anything. But I'll be looking forward to that."

I nod. "So. Goodbye hug?"

Erin nods and we stand there for a minute, hugging each other tightly, my head on their shoulder one last time.

And then I walk away, and I don't let myself look back.

I meet up with Mark, Paige, Babs, and Shirley, who all look hot and tired but very happy. Paige doesn't stop talking for literally half an hour: from the time we get into the car until we are back on the highway and heading north, she recites every

227

single amazing thing she has seen. The giant rainbow flag. The man wearing the blue-and-silver wings made of actual feathers. The Dalmatian with rainbow spots and the Chihuahua wearing a tiara. The girl with the rainbow unicorn horn on her head.

Finally, Mark cuts her off. "Paige. Enough already. We were all there, remember?"

But she's unstoppable. "And the girls on the bicycles with no shirts on! I wish I didn't have to wear a shirt. Why do I, anyway?"

"You don't," I say. "There's no law that says you have to. Not in Ontario, anyway."

Paige just gives me the disdainful look that my comment deserves, and moves on. "Oh, and I saw these people with a big sign that said . . . um—" She glances at Shirley. "—That said 'EFF the gender binary.'" She giggles, presumably at her own audacity in almost swearing. "And also, there was this guy juggling. And he was amazing. I mean, it was ALL amazing."

I grin and nod. She's right. It was all amazing. I sneak a sideways peek at Mark and find him watching me.

"Glad we went?" he says.

I nod. "So glad. So, so, so glad."

"You're welcome," he says.

Babs and Shirley drive us to their friend's garage, where we pick up the Mustang—*Grandma's* Mustang, I remind myself. I'm still annoyed that I assumed it was Grandpa's.

Babs's mechanic friend replaces the damaged part while we wait, and just like that, it's running fine. Her friend waves away our payment, but I bet Babs is picking up the tab herself. "You three want to come back to our place for a bite to eat?" Shirley asks.

Mark shakes his head. "We should get back. It's still a bit of a drive."

"Aww," Paige pouts, probably remembering all the ice cream she ate at their house last time.

"Well, I guess this is it, then," Babs says, slapping the hood of the Mustang. "Safe travels, kids."

We hug them goodbye, and Paige gets a bit teary, but Shirley just tells her to cut out the waterworks: "It's not like we're never going to see you again," she says. "You get in touch next summer, when you're back at the cottage."

"We will," Mark says. "Promise."

We drive away, waving, but my mind is already skipping ahead. When we're back here next summer—*if* we're back here—will it be to sell the cottage? Will Grandma make it up for one last visit? Will my dad and Janet even be on speaking terms?

I push the thoughts away. Mark, Paige, and I have at least a couple of days in Muskoka together before we get dragged back to opposite ends of the country. I'm going to make the most of them.

The sun is setting by the time we arrive at the cottage: fiery orange spilling out from under the clouds and lighting up the surface of the lake. The three of us sit down on the dock, watching the colors shift and change, and slapping at the mosquitoes.

I slip off my sandals and dangle my feet over the water. "Want to go for a swim?" I ask.

Mark shakes his head. "There's a lot to do."

"Not tonight," I protest. "Seriously?" I give him a shove—not hard enough to make him fall in, but hard enough to make him shove me back. And when he does, I don't resist—I just hold on to his arm so that he's coming in with me.

The shock of the cold water is enough to make me gasp, and as I surface, I hear Mark's laughter and Paige's outraged shriek: I guess our splash soaked her.

And then I hear a voice: "Well, look who's back!"

I tread water, flipping my hair out of my eyes. "Mariana?"

"Hey. Where'd you guys disappear to?"

"Toronto," I say. "For Pride weekend. It was kind of . . . unplanned."

Mark snorts, pulls himself up onto the dock, and wraps his arms around himself. "Freezing, freezing, oh my god."

Mariana looks around. "No towels?"

"Swimming was also kind of unplanned," he says.

"I'm all wet," Paige says. "And I didn't even go in the water, and now I'm getting cold. And I've already got about ten mosquito bites."

"I guess we're heading back to the cottage," I say. "Want to join us?"

———

We turn on the lights and find towels, leaving a trail of drips and wet footprints from the front door to the linen closet. I wrap a big blue towel around myself, over my wet clothes, and plug in the kettle. "You want tea, Mariana? Or hot chocolate? Or there's beer in the fridge."

"Hot chocolate would be great, actually." She plops down on the couch.

"I'm just going to get dry clothes," I say. "Be right back."

In my tiny room, I strip off my wet things, towel myself off, and pull on a pair of flannel pants and an old T-shirt. As I turn to leave, I catch a glimpse of myself in the round mirror that hangs on the door: a mess of damp, tangled curls, a face that's freckled and flushed from a day in the sun, and a wide grin for no reason at all. My *Queer Pride* sticker has survived its dip in the lake. I peel it off and stick it to the side of my suitcase: have Pride, will travel.

When I come back out into the living room, Mark and Paige are sitting on either side of Mariana, who's flipping through the photo album that Paige and I found, the one labeled *Bracebridge Summer Days: Janet, Gary, and Frank, the "honorary Tremblay."*

"This is amazing," she says. "It's hard to believe our parents were ever this young. And that they were friends!"

"There's a photo from every year from when they were little until when they were teens," I say, leaning over from behind the couch to look.

Mariana looks back at the photo. "They're all, like, our age. So weird." She flips through the album and tries to make sense of things. "So your mom," she says, looking at Mark and Paige, then turns to me, "and your dad, are brother and sister, and they're here in Ontario together, but they aren't really on speaking terms?"

"They speak," I say. "It's just not all that friendly. The only reason we're here in the first place is because our grandpa died, and our grandmother asked us all to come and figure out what to do with the cottage."

"Yeah," says Mark. "She gave them a major guilt trip. If it weren't for that, I don't think we'd be here at all. Not as a family, anyway."

"I've never been here," says Paige.

"Yeah, you have," says Mark. "You just don't remember."

"Same thing," she says, shrugging.

"We used to spend family vacations here until Mark and I were about ten," I explain. "All of us. Then it just kind of . . . stopped."

Mariana stares down at the photo that's open on her lap. Mom, Gary, and Frank at about sixteen, all damp hair and bathing suits, beaming at the camera from the end of the dock with their arms slung over each other's shoulders. "They were obviously super close," she says. "Dad made it sound like . . . like, oh yeah, we used to know each other when we were kids. But it looks more like he was practically part of your family."

I shrug. "I guess. A million years ago."

"I just think it's so weird that I've never heard of any of you."

"It's like your dad told us," I say. "They just grew apart. I guess when you're young you make all these plans to stay tight with your friends, to stay in touch, but I don't think it's always that easy."

"I don't know," says Mariana. "It just feels like there has to be more to it than that."

CHAPTER TWENTY-SEVEN

MARK

My phone begins to vibrate in my pocket. I pull it out and check the display.

"It's Mom," I say, stepping out onto the deck to answer it.

"Hey," I say.

"Mark," she says. "How's everything up there?"

"Great," I say. "We've been cleaning all afternoon and just stopped to barbecue something for supper. How are you? You sound tired."

She laughs. "Is it that obvious? Yeah, I'm exhausted, it's been a long week, but the good news is that Grandma is out of the hospital, and it looks like she'll be able to stay in her condo, at least for the time being. Gary managed to find some in-home care for her, a nurse who will stop by once a day, and a nice young man who will come in the mornings and the evenings to help with meals and make sure she's doing all right."

"That's great!" I say.

"Your grandmother is happy," says Mom. She doesn't sound quite as enthusiastic, however. "It's hard to know what to think, to be honest. Gary and I both agree that she'd be better off in a full-time care facility, but she wants to live on her own for now. It might not be such a big deal if one or both of us lived closer to Toronto, but she won't consider moving to either coast."

"It'll be okay, Mom," I say. I can't think of anything else to say. Mom doesn't usually unload this kind of adult stuff on me. Through the window, I can see the girls sitting around, staring out at me, wondering what we're talking about.

"Yes," says Mom, her voice returning to its usual efficient, practical tone. "The bottom line is that your grandmother is an adult, and there's not much to be done when she's made up her mind. Which is the reason I'm calling. It looks like the three of us are going to be coming up to Muskoka tomorrow."

"Grandma too?" I ask. "Really?"

She sighs. "She's being quite insistent about it, and the doctor gave her the go-ahead. He'd prefer she stay in the city, but he says that as long as she spends her time relaxing, it should be okay. Gary thinks the fresh air might actually do her some good, and, to be honest, I kind of agree."

"Sounds like you and Gary are doing lots of agreeing," I say.

"Don't start, Mark," she warns. "Anyway, we should arrive midafternoon. Try to stick close to the cottage. I know Grandma is really excited to see the three of you."

"We will," I promise. I don't ask if they're driving together, since it feels like I'd be pushing my luck.

After I hang up, I go back inside and pass along the news.

"Maybe we'll finally get to the bottom of things," says Paige.

We spend the morning hustling like crazy, trying to make it look like we've at least tackled a good chunk of the work that they left for us. Before they arrive, I warn Paige not to bring up Frank with Mom and Gary.

"Why not?" she whines.

"Because Grandma hasn't been here all year," I tell her. "Let's give her a chance to get settled before we dig into family drama."

They arrive a couple of hours after lunch, and the three of us walk out to greet them like a group of servants from *Downton Abbey*, waving excitedly as the car comes down the lane. Gary is driving, and when he parks, Mom gets out of the backseat and goes around to help Grandma out of the passenger side.

Grandma is noticeably frailer than she was just over a week ago when she was cooking a turkey and bossing Mom and Gary around. She's smiling broadly, though, stopping to lift her face and smell the air, before opening her arms toward us, beckoning us forward for hugs.

"You probably want to go in and have a nap, Mom," says Gary.

"Are you kidding me?" she says. "Not before I get a ride around the lake with my grandkids. I haven't been in the Mustang for years, and I've been missing her something fierce."

Gary and Mom exchange glances. "You know what the doctor said," says Mom. "You've got to take it easy. That's the only reason you're here."

"I'll take it easy when I'm dead, Janet," says Grandma. "Mark, do you want to drive?"

I look at Mom, who just shakes her head, frustrated, and heads inside with her bags.

Gary turns to me, and I can tell that he knows it's no use arguing. "Go slow, and don't let her boss you into going any farther than the marina. Capiche?"

I'm not sure who chatters more as we meander around the lake, Paige or Grandma. Grandma points out the window at cottages, getting excited when she recognizes the names on the mailboxes, clucking disapprovingly at the newer, more ostentatious places that have popped up in recent years. Paige has a million questions about what the lake was like when Grandma was younger, if they had different flavors of ice cream back then, whether or not there were paddleboats.

When we pass the cottage where Mariana is staying with her father, Paige leans forward with sly purpose.

"What were Mom and Gary like when they were kids?" she asks.

"Paige," I say warningly. She ignores me, and Grandma doesn't seem to notice.

"Your mother was a great swimmer," says Grandma. "She always had lots of friends. Gary was a bit more reserved, but he loved the cottage. He always arrived with a big stack of books every summer. They both loved going out in the canoe in the early mornings. We all did, your grandfather most of all." Her voice is wistful, and she turns to stare out the window toward the lake.

Paige, however, doesn't pick up on the solemn vibe. "What about Frank? Did Frank like going out in the canoe?" she asks in her most innocent voice.

Grandma turns to look at her.

"Yes," she says. "Frank and Gary did pretty much everything together, and your mother tagged along with them as much as they'd let her."

Paige slumps back into her seat. It's clear that she was hoping for a more satisfying clue for her mystery.

I pull into the marina parking lot and turn off the car, and we stare out at the boats.

"I can't think of a better way to spend my last stay at the cottage than out on a joyride with my grandchildren," says Grandma after a moment.

"What do you mean?" asks Paige. "You're going to come back every summer for years. You said. You said it at the hospital."

"Yes," says Grandma. "I certainly did say that. I misspoke."

Paige seems satisfied, turning her attention back to the ice cream stand nearby, but I can tell from Grandma's voice that she means it. She doesn't expect to be back to the cottage again after this. I glance in the rearview mirror and catch Talia's eye, and I can tell that she's come to the same conclusion.

Without warning, my throat gets tight, and I feel my eyes well up a little. I reach over and put my hand on Grandma's, and a second later, I feel Talia reach forward and put her hand on top of mine.

"Can we come back for supper?" asks Paige, oblivious to everything.

"I think that sounds like a grand idea," says Grandma. "I'm craving some seafood. Now, if we can just persuade those stick-in-the-mud parents of yours."

"I'll persuade them," says Paige. "I've got ways."

———

It actually isn't hard to convince Mom and Gary at all. When we arrive back at the cottage, they're sitting out on the deck together, chatting and looking out at the lake. It occurs to me that Talia and I might not be the only ones to have done some soul-searching over the past week.

We take turns getting washed up in the tiny bathroom, and then change into what counts as fancy for dinner in cottage country. I pull on my khakis and a button-up, and when I come out of my bedroom, I see that Talia's wearing a sort of linen sundress with a cool hippie-looking print. She looks light and happy in a way that I haven't seen from her before.

"You look great," I say.

"Don't sound so surprised," she says. "I feel great. I'm really happy that Grandma could make it after all."

When everyone else is ready, Grandma wants us all to cram into the Mustang, but Mom won't hear of it—not enough seat belts—so we caravan our way toward the restaurant. We find ourselves a table on the deck, looking out at the water. It's a beautiful evening, the temperature is perfect, the lake is calm and beautiful, and soon we're sharing some calamari and telling stories. Talia and I fill Grandma in on our wild Pride adventure, Grandma has her own memories to share, and best of all, Mom and Gary begin to talk about when they were kids at the cottage. Soon, we're all laughing, and actually behaving like a real family. A family that gets along.

It's a perfect end to a great day until I see Mom look past me, and her eyes wide as she smiles. "Frank?" she calls. "My goodness. I can't believe it!"

I turn and see that Mariana and her father have stepped onto the deck, just a few feet from us.

Gary pushes his chair back. "Well, well," he says. I can't help noticing that he sounds a whole lot less happy than my mom does.

CHAPTER TWENTY-EIGHT

TALIA

I can see a muscle twitching in my dad's jaw as Frank and Mariana walk toward us. Guess this was a friendship that didn't end well; though Janet looks happy enough.

Paige is oblivious. She's studying her menu. "Ooh," she says, her voice startlingly loud. "They have tiramisu!"

Grandma clears her throat. "Such a lovely evening," she says. "Who wants to go for a little walk? Paige?"

Paige shakes her head. "And hot fudge brownies with ice cream," she says. "Can we get dessert?" She looks up at Janet. "Mom?"

Janet puts down her water glass and lifts a hand to wave to Frank. He waves back. Dad mutters something that sounds an awful lot like *hoo boy*.

I smile at Mariana. "Hey."

"Hi, Talia," she says.

"Hello, Frank," Janet says.

"Long time no see," he says, and I wince: I really wish people would not use that expression.

"We're just finishing up," Janet says, gesturing at the empty plates. "But if you'd like to join us for a drink? It looks like our kids have already met . . ."

"Thank you." Frank clears his throat. "Actually, I met your kids last week. Mariana invited them round for a barbecue. That's how I found out you guys were here."

Janet looks at Mark, Paige, and me. "The three of us were best friends when we were growing up. But it was a long time ago."

"Ancient history," Frank says. "You know, our kids are the same age that we were when we last saw each other."

"You're right," Janet says. "Almost exactly the same age we were that summer."

Dad doesn't say anything, and I can see that muscle twitching in his jaw again.

"Well!" Grandma says. "Paige, how about you and I go for ice cream across the street? And Mark, Talia, Mariana . . . do you want to join us? Let these three catch up on the last twenty-odd years?"

"Sure," I say, somewhat reluctantly.

I'd really like to listen in, but I can take a hint.

While Paige and Grandma head into the ice cream shop, Mariana, Mark, and I wander along the docks in search of a private spot to sit and talk. We plunk ourselves at the end of slip, beside a moored powerboat called, disturbingly, *Wet Dream*. I swat at a mosquito on my arm and turn to the others. "So. Wow. That was awkward."

"No shit." Mark looks at Mariana. "Do you have any idea what the story is with our parents?"

Mariana nods. "After I saw that photo album of the three of them, I asked my dad to tell me the whole story."

"And?"

"Your dad and my dad were friends for years, Dad said. As far back as he remembers. Their families both had cottages close by and they spent all July and August together. Janet too, but she was a year younger, and a girl, so she was . . . I guess she tagged along? Like, sometimes they were a trio, but my dad and Gary were totally best friends."

"And then what? They had some kind of fight? Or . . ."

Mariana looks uncomfortable. "Uh, this is kind of weird to say, but my dad and Janet hooked up. When they were, like, seventeen and eighteen, Dad said. But they didn't tell Gary because . . . I don't know exactly. Dad said he figured Gary wouldn't like the idea of his best friend hooking up with his little sister, so they kept it a secret."

I'm picturing the three of them as they looked in that last photo: standing on the end of the dock, arms around each other, suntanned and grinning. Just three friends, I'd thought. It would've been the early nineties, and Janet was wearing short denim overalls and a spiral perm. Frank and Gary stood on either side of her, towering over her. Her secret boyfriend and her overprotective big brother.

"It's so weird to think of our parents being our age," Mark says out loud. "So weird to think of them having all that drama."

"Yeah, but this was over twenty years ago," I say. "Did my dad find out? Is that why they stopped being friends?"

Mark leans forward. "Yeah. Did it all end really badly or what?"

Mariana shrugs. "Nope. Dad and Janet broke up, and they all just drifted apart. Went to university, got jobs, stopped coming to the cottage. No big mystery. Just life."

"I guess," Mark says. "Still . . . imagine if something crazy happened with the three of us, and then we didn't see each other for twenty-whatever years? And we were all in our forties and had teenage kids?" He shudders. "What a horrible thought."

I laugh. "Which part?"

"All of it."

"Maybe you'll run into Darren in the way-off future," I say, and I fill Mariana in on what happened.

"What an asshole," she says. "I'm not even surprised."

"I bet he'll be bald at forty," Mark says.

"Twice divorced," I say.

"With a beer gut," Mark adds, and he grins at me.

CHAPTER TWENTY-NINE

MARK

When we leave the restaurant, Mom, Paige, and I drive home in the rental, while Grandma, Talia, and Gary follow in the Mustang. When we get home, I slip out and walk down to the lake.

I sit on the edge of the dock, dangling my feet in the water, thinking back to the day, less than two weeks ago, that we first flew to Ontario. All I could think about on the plane was how bold and huge and dramatic Toronto was going to be, how epic Pride would be. I was wondering how to take advantage of the situation, thinking about how the real world was waiting to emerge from a cloud and open up to envelop me. I was only concerned with the things that would happen to me. I wasn't concerned about how I was going to behave or react.

Grandpa had died, and although I was sad, in an "oh man, that sucks that Grandpa died" kind of way, I don't think I'd really thought about what it meant. Grandpa, to me, was a nice old guy who used to take me out on the canoe, and then showed up for Christmas every couple of years. But to Mom and Gary and Grandma, he was a whole lot more than that.

I hear footsteps rustle through the brush, and then steps, light and hollow, on the dock. A moment later, my mother sits down next to me.

"What a night," she says, looking out at the lake. She reaches over to put an arm around my shoulder. "How are you doing, sweetie?"

"Mom," I say, letting myself lean in to her hug. "I'm sorry about Grandpa." The last word comes out just halfway, hollow and sad, and I close my eyes against a wash of tears.

My mother just pulls me a bit closer, her hand sliding up my arm to my head, pulling it tighter, down onto hers. She doesn't speak for a moment, then I feel her nod.

"I know, Mark. I know you are. I miss him a lot."

I sniff and pull back, bending my arms back and stretching them behind me, releasing a puff of breath. I wipe my eyes with the back of my hand, pulling myself together. "I'm sorry if I've been difficult on this trip. I spent too much time thinking about how this should be fun for me, and not thinking about how shitty it was for you and Gary and Grandma. I mean, it was shitty for us, too, but, I mean, he was your *dad.*"

She smiles and reaches out to rub my arm.

"I understand, sweetie," she says. "Don't beat yourself up."

246

"Mariana told us about you and Frank," I say. "About what happened that summer."

"It was a long time ago," she says. "It's hard to believe that I was your age that year."

"Was it weird," I ask, "seeing him again?"

"It was a bit of a surprise," she says. "I hadn't thought about him in years. But it was kind of nice, too. Frank was my first boyfriend. Seeing him made me think of myself at that age, of the way we used to look at each other." She smiles, and her eyes drift off as she remembers.

"Is Frank the reason that you and Gary stopped talking?" I ask.

She sighs. "Yes and no. It's kind of a long story."

"I've got time."

"The truth is," she says, "Gary and Frank were best friends for years. Frank's family owned a cottage nearby, and he was always around in the summers. 'The honorary Tremblay' is pretty accurate. They were inseparable, and, of course, I was around because I was the kid sister, and they couldn't really get rid of me. But then we all grew up a little bit."

"And you and Frank hooked up," I say.

She nods. "It just kind of happened, and we realized we really liked each other. The only problem was Gary. We didn't know how to tell him, so we decided not to. Frank was worried that he'd be upset that his best friend was hooking up with his little sister. I knew better, though. I knew Gary would really be hurt and jealous, and angry at me for taking Frank away from him. In any case, we decided it was best to keep it a secret."

"That must have been hard to keep up," I say.

She laughs. "Oh, yeah. It was kind of crazy. We made a game of it, and that became the story of the summer. 'Our secret romance.' It was fun, dramatic. The problem was, we didn't really think about how it would affect Gary. All he knew was that Frank had pretty much stopped hanging out with him, and I guess he just assumed I was off with my other friends. I was always really social, but Gary didn't have a lot of friends. He was quiet and serious. Talia reminds me of him a lot, to be honest. He'd always loved the cottage because he knew that his best buddy Frank would be there, and then he didn't have that anymore."

"And you never told him what happened?" I ask.

She shakes her head. "The summer ended and we all went our separate ways. Then Gary went to college that fall, and one thing led to another, and there was never a really good opportunity to tell him. The next summer, we arrived to learn that Frank's family had sold their cottage. For all those years, he honestly thought that Frank had bailed on him. Then one night, years later when you and Talia were just kids, and Paige was barely a toddler, I let something slip when we were here at the cottage. We'd been bickering all week, and I don't really remember how it came out, but it was really the straw that broke the camel's back. Gary completely lost it, and we ended up having a huge fight, and . . ." She makes an expression with her hands, like dust being released into the wind.

"So that's why you and Gary haven't spoken in so long?"

She nods. "It all sounds so ridiculous now, when I tell the story out loud. But Gary was really hurt when he found out, and we both said some ugly things. Maybe if we'd lived closer, it would have been easier to mend it. But out of sight, out of mind, I guess. One year turned into two, then five, then seven, and here we are . . ."

"Do you think things might change now?" I ask.

She laughs, lightly. "The funny thing is, it really started to feel like they might, over the past few days. Gary and I have actually been talking. We went out for dinner one night, just to get away from the hospital, and ended up staying out, drinking some wine . . . And then Frank showed up and everything got dragged up again. We'll see what happens."

"Well, for what it's worth," I say, standing and reaching down to give her a hand, "Paige and Talia and I vote to keep the cottage."

"You've decided as a group, then?" she asks. "A Tremblay-grandchild voting bloc?"

"Yup. Never underestimate the power of a strategic alliance," I say.

She laughs and links her arm with mine, and we walk back up the hill to the cottage. When we walk up the steps onto the deck, I see that Gary is sitting on one of the Muskoka chairs with a glass of wine, staring out at the twilit lake. He twists around to look at us as we step onto the deck.

"There's a bottle open in there, Janet," he says. "If you want to grab a glass."

She smiles. "I might just do that."

Inside, Paige is collapsed on Grandpa's giant, overstuffed armchair, practically hanging upside down with her book in front of her face. Talia is on the sofa, looking at her phone.

"Technology," I say, flopping onto couch next to her. "A terrible substitute for conversation."

I can tell that Talia is holding back a grin, and she continues to stubbornly swipe her touch screen.

"I thought you were supposed to be a total West Coast granola," I say. "Aren't you sending bad vibes into my karma or whatever?"

This time she does laugh. She puts down her phone and grabs a pillow, whipping it at me from across the couch. "You're a pest, do you know that?"

"He *is* a pest!" exclaims Paige from behind her book.

I grab the pillow and squeeze it close to me, hugging it like I'm a little kid with a teddy bear. "You guys wanna play Truth or Dare?" I ask.

"I'm not in the mood for any more truths, Mark," says Talia. "I'm all truthed out for the time being."

A burst of laughter comes at us from outside. Paige flips right side up in her chair, and the three of us turn to stare out the window. Out on the deck, Gary is turned toward Mom, animatedly telling her a story, his arms gesticulating wildly. Mom's head is rolled back, and she's laughing out loud.

"Holy shit," I say.

"What is going on?" asks Paige.

"Looks like we might see each other again before seven years," says Talia.

CHAPTER THIRTY

TALIA

That night, I can't sleep. Not because I'm worrying about any of the usual dozen things that keep me awake at night, but just because my brain is so full. I'm mostly happy: happy that Janet and Dad seem to have reconnected, happy that I've spent this time with Mark and Paige. I'm even moderately okay-ish about how things are with me and Erin. But there's a weird undercurrent of restlessness under all that happy. Soon Dad and I will be flying home, and the future feels like a great big blank canvas.

Which might be great if I were an artist, but blank canvasses are not my thing. As much as I wish I could just be excited about all the wide-open possibilities, the truth is, I like to have plans. Detailed, highlighted, bullet-pointed plans.

I sit up, pick up my jeans from where I'd left them on the floor, and pull them back on. I'm about to open my bedroom door when someone knocks on it, very softly.

I open the door. "Mark?"

"I can't sleep," he says.

I laugh. "Me neither. I just gave up, actually."

"Want to go for a walk?"

I nod. "Let's go."

———

We walk down the short trail to the lake. The sky above the tall trees is clear and star-studded. Mark stops, pulls a blanket out of his bag, and spreads it out on the beach with a flourish. "Take a seat."

I laugh and sit cross-legged, looking out at the dark, glassy water. Mark drops down beside me and lies back, propped up on his elbows. A perfect Muskoka night. Back home, Erin and I used to go sit on the beach at night, but this is totally different: calm lake instead of ocean waves, warm air instead of a chilly breeze, and the kind of quiet you never really experience in the city. Also mosquitos: I slap at one that's hovering around my ankle, but miss.

Neither of us says anything for a few minutes, and it's a comfortable sort of silence. Finally, Mark lets out a contented sigh. "I'm glad we're not selling this place."

"Same," I say. "I'm glad we're coming back."

"Yeah. It seems like our parents are managing to get along again," he says.

I nod. "And I'm glad that Grandma is back at the cottage."

He laughs. "What is this, Thanksgiving dinner? Are you counting our blessings now?"

I laugh, too, but I guess I am in a grateful kind of mood. "Yeah, kind of."

"In that case, can I just say that I think it's pretty awesome that we made it to Pride after all? Against the odds?"

"You know, none of that would have happened if Darren hadn't turned out to be such an asshole," I say.

Mark rolls onto his side to face me. "I hope you aren't expecting me to count him as a blessing, Talia."

"Nah. He's just a jerk. Now, Jeremy, on the other hand . . ."

Mark's face lights up—he can't hide how he feels about this guy, and it makes me happy. "Yes! And he's moving to the East Coast. I still can't believe how lucky that is. You know, I feel like the trip to Toronto was meant to happen."

I don't believe in fate. It is weird, though, to think that any little thing could have gone differently and none of this would have happened. If we hadn't caught Darren stealing, if Mark hadn't tried to take off, if the car hadn't broken down, if meeting Mariana hadn't brought Frank back onto the scene and forced our parents to deal with the past . . . Mark wouldn't have met Jeremy. The cottage might be sold. And Erin and I might still be stuck in that awful limbo . . .

"And now you're happily single instead of moping around, staring at your phone." He looks at me. "Or was that totally insensitive? Crap. It was, wasn't it? I'm sorry. I guess it's way too soon to celebrate that."

"Nah, it's okay." I pick up a stone and hold it in my hand, cool and smooth and heavy. "Actually, it's kind of interesting to think about, you know? Not that I'm in any hurry to meet anyone, but it's sort of . . . well, it's interesting to think that I could. You know. Maybe." For some reason, I find myself remembering the bird-tattooed cutie I bumped into outside Erin's coffee shop.

"You're blushing," Mark says.

"I know." I blush at everything; it's absurd and embarrassing. "Anyway . . ."

"Changing the subject?" He grins. "Okay. What are you going to do for the summer?"

I make a face. July and August stretch out ahead, and I'm supposed to be starting at the university in the fall, but . . . "I have to find a job, I guess."

"Yeah. Me too." He grins. "Preferably one that leaves me with lots of time for soccer and Jeremy."

"Do you have something lined up?"

He shrugs. "The soccer camp near my house could probably use help, with the kids, you know? Coaching or whatever."

"I've never really had a job," I say. "Not, like, a proper one. Just babysitting and stuff like that."

"Seriously? I've had jobs every summer and most weekends since I was, like, fourteen."

"Dad wanted me to focus on school work, so . . ."

"You probably got way better grades than me."

"Straight As, always. But that makes me nervous, too. About starting university, I mean."

"You'll do fine."

"Yeah." I look sideways at him. "I feel like I've been kind of doing what everyone expects, you know? Dad mostly, but Erin, too. Even my mom—not coming out to her, I mean. Letting her think I'm straight. And I'm not sure . . . I'm not sure what *I* want to do." I take a deep breath. "I don't know if I even want to go to university in the fall. But I can't imagine telling my dad that."

Mark actually laughs. "It's not that big of a deal. Just say you're going to defer it a year, take some time to explore other possibilities. It's not like you're telling him you've decided to become a . . . I don't know, a burlesque dancer."

"I guess not." I make a face at him. "I was thinking of maybe getting a job and saving some money, then traveling a bit. Or getting a job somewhere other than Victoria. But I don't really have a plan yet . . ."

"If you want to stop doing what everyone expects, you have to start somewhere."

"I know." I look at the stone in my hands for a few seconds, and then toss it at the water. It skips: one, two, three, four times.

"Hey, I can never do that."

"There you go," he says. "You're already shattering expectations."

The next morning, Dad and Janet cook up a big pancake breakfast for everyone, talking and laughing together while they work. Paige dances around in her pajamas, singing some little kid song about pancakes "with berries that are blue." Grandma sits on the couch looking tired but content. She pats the seat beside her, beckoning me to sit.

"How are you doing?" I ask. I feel a bit shy with her—the truth is, I don't really know her very well at all. I wish we hadn't missed those seven years at the cottage. I wish Dad and Janet hadn't taken so long to get over their stupid fight. I wish I'd come to visit my grandparents when Dad did, instead of making excuses, saying I was too busy, being so wrapped up in my own life. I hadn't really thought about the fact that they wouldn't always be there.

"Very well indeed," she says. She nods toward Mark, who is setting the table. "You two seem to get on like a house on fire."

I laugh. "Yeah. Well, not at first, actually. But yeah. I guess we got pretty close over the last few days."

"You get along better than your parents ever did," she says, and sighs.

"When they were kids, even? They used to fight?"

"Oh, constantly. Always jealous of each other, always bickering. Gary could be awfully bossy, mind you. Always so sure he was right. And, well, a bit sensitive."

"So it was all his fault?" I ask, feeling suddenly protective.

"Oh, no, no, not at all. Janet wasn't always easy. Gary was rather shy and didn't make friends easily, but she was a social butterfly. And she—well, she probably didn't mean to rub it in his face, but she was just a grade behind him and she was a bit self-absorbed. I suppose most kids are."

I try to picture my dad as an awkward high school student with an annoyingly popular little sister, but I can't imagine it.

"I suppose every parent wishes their children would be best of friends," Grandma says. "Soon I'll be gone and those two will be all the family that's left. That should count for something, don't you think?"

I have a lump in my throat. "You're not going anywhere," I say. "We'll all be back here together next summer."

"Maybe we will," she says, patting my leg.

"Grub's up!" Mark yells.

I get to my feet and hold out a hand to help Grandma up. She takes it, and stands with some difficulty, giving a little grunt of effort. "Getting old is not for the weak, Talia. But it beats the alternative, as they say."

"I guess it does."

We make our way over to the table and Mark pulls out a chair for Grandma with a flourish. "Madam."

She sits down. "Thank you, sir."

Paige giggles. "Sir?"

Mark gives her a gentle shove. "Hey, why not? You could stand to have a little more respect for your elders."

Gales of laughter at that one. Mark looks at Grandma and rolls his eyes. "See what I have to put up with?"

She just smiles. "Your biggest fan, that one. She worships the ground you walk on."

"I do NOT!" Paige says.

But I think Grandma just nailed it.

The grown-ups linger over coffee, but Paige is restless, so she, Mark, and I head up to the loft to play Jenga. It reminds me of old times: being up here with Mark, years ago, playing with these same wooden blocks.

"Who gets the Jenga if the cottage gets sold?" I joke out loud.

"It's not getting sold," Paige says. "Grandma said it's a family decision, and there are three of us, so we can outvote them."

I hope she's right. In my experience, kids' votes aren't always given equal weight.

"There are three grown-ups, too," Mark points out.

"Yeah, but Grandma's on our side," Paige says with great certainty.

I think she's right about that: I'm just not sure how much it will matter. "We need to persuade Dad and your mom," I say. "They're the ones who'll really decide."

Mark slides out a Jenga block and the tower wobbles but doesn't fall. "Did you talk to your dad? About university and stuff?"

I shake my head. "Not yet. But I'm going to. Today."

He high-fives me.

"What?" Paige says. "Talk to your dad about what?"

"Just some stuff about traveling in the fall," I say.

"Come visit us," Paige says.

"I might do that."

"I told Grandma to visit us, too," Paige says. "So she can meet Mark's new boyfriend."

Mark and I both stare at her, then look at each other. "Uh, you told Grandma about Jeremy?" Mark says.

Of course she did.

"Yeah. And she wants to meet him."

"So . . . Grandma was cool with it?" I ask.

Paige looks at me like I'm stupid. "Why wouldn't she be?"

"You're kind of awesome, Paige," I say.

"I know," Paige says, and we all laugh.

After breakfast, Dad and I do the dishes together while Mark and Paige start a game of Monopoly. Janet and Grandma sit out on the deck playing cards and talking.

"It's been quite a week," Dad says. "Are you doing okay, Talia? I've been so wrapped up in dealing with the hospital and making plans for my mother, I feel like we've hardly spoken. I know you saw Erin . . ."

"Yeah. It's okay."

"You two are still together?"

"No. No, we broke up." I rinse the glass in my hands, stick it in the dish rack, and dry my hands off on my shorts. "But I'm okay with it. I think . . . it's the way it needed to be, I guess."

He nods. "I'll miss Erin. I'm sure you will, too. But high school romances rarely last. Your mother and I . . . well, we got together at eighteen, and look how that ended up."

I look at him sideways. He never talks about my mother.

"People change," he says. "It happens. Though no regrets: if we'd broken up when we should've, there'd be no Talia."

I think about that for a minute. I don't have regrets about going out with Erin. Like, I don't feel like our whole relationship was a mistake or anything like that. I just never thought it would end like this. I never really thought it would end at all.

There's a lump in my throat, and I have to force the words past it. "It's just . . . Erin was my best friend," I say. "For years. Not just my partner."

"I know," Dad says. "I know."

"I don't even have other friends," I say. "Not close ones. I told Erin *everything*. Even when I'm feeling sad about breaking up with them, the only person I want to talk to about that is . . ."

"Erin," he says. "I know, love."

There's a long silence. He rubs my back and I lean against him, staring out the window over the sink.

"It'll get easier," he says. "Eventually. And you will make other friends."

I snort.

"Well . . . eventually," he says and laughs a little. "Sometimes I think you're too much like me, Talia."

"What do you mean?" I pull away and look at him. "You say that like it's a bad thing."

"I don't mean it that way." He tilts his head, his eyes on mine. "You're wonderful, Talia, and I wouldn't change a thing about you. You are a loving, loyal friend. You've always been the kind of person who'd rather have one real, deep friendship than a big group of acquaintances. And that's not a bad thing at all. But when you lose a friendship like that . . . well, it's a big loss."

"Like Frank," I say.

He nods. "Yeah. Like Frank. But life goes on." He fishes some stray pieces of cutlery from under the soapy surface and wipes each off with a cloth.

I take a deep breath. "Um. Dad?"

"Yes?"

"I've been thinking."

"Uh oh." He turns to face me, his hands deep in the soapy water.

I make a face at him. "Seriously."

"Okay. Seriously. What is it?" His forehead is creased. "Talk to me."

"I . . . I don't think I want to go to university in the fall."

"You don't?"

I shake my head. "I'm just going because . . . I don't even know why. I just assumed that was what came next, you know?"

"Well, it is, usually . . ."

"But there's no point in going and spending all that money and time if I don't even want to be there. I don't even know what I want to study."

"So you take a bunch of different classes. Try things out." Dad takes his hands out of the sink and dries them on a towel. "University can be a good way to find out what you want to do."

"An expensive way," I say.

"We can afford it."

"I know. And I appreciate the support. But what if . . ." I hesitate, then plow on. "What if I worked for a while and saved some money? And did some traveling?"

"By yourself?"

"Yeah. By myself."

"Where would you go?"

"Haven't decided yet." I feel a bone-deep buzz of excitement. Of possibility. "I mean, I'll make a solid plan," I say quickly. "I'm not just going to take off. Or, you know, just bum around."

Dad laughs. "I wasn't worried about that, Talia," he says. "Nothing wrong with taking some time for yourself."

"Really?"

"Of course."

"You're not . . . disappointed?"

He looks taken aback and maybe slightly offended. "Of course not. I just want you to be happy."

I throw my arms around him and give him a massive hug.

We are just finishing up with the dishes when Grandma and Janet come back inside. There is something very decisive about Grandma's pose: hands on her hips, chin raised.

"Can everyone please come to the living room?" she calls out.

I dry my hands as Mark and Paige scramble down the ladder and the adults take seats on the couch and chairs. There's a heavy sense of expectation in the air: before Grandma even begins, I know what she's going to say.

"I was going to wait until we'd been here a few days," Grandma says. "But I think I'd enjoy this more if we just got this decision out of the way. You all know how I feel: I want my children and my grandchildren to go on enjoying this special place. It gives me great pleasure to think that maybe someday Mark or Talia or Paige will have a child, and that child will swim in the lake and play board games in the loft and climb these same trees that my children climbed." Her eyes are watery but she is smiling. "But the truth is, none of that really matters, because I suspect this will be my last visit. So it is up to all of you to decide about the future. Shall we sell this place? Or do you want to take over the upkeep?"

"Well," Dad starts.

"The thing is . . ." Janet says.

"I want to keep it!" Paige shouts.

Grandma shakes her head. "Halifax and Victoria are a long way away," she says. "And if this isn't what you want to do with your summers, I don't want you to feel any pressure."

"Maybe we should vote," Paige says. "I say yes. We keep it." She sticks a hand straight up in the air, waving it over her head. "Who's with me? Who votes YES to keeping the cottage?"

I raise my hand. Mark raises his hand.

"Grandma, you can vote," Paige says.

"I'm abstaining," she says.

We all turn to Janet and Dad, who are looking at each other.

"Please say yes," Paige whispers.

Janet and Dad both start to laugh. "Yes," Janet says, and they both raise their hands. "If you all would've let us get a word in, we'd have told you that we talked about this last night and decided to give it a go. To keep the cottage, at least for now."

Paige punches the air. "YES!"

"Not promising that it'll still be here for your children," Gary says. "But how about we all come back next summer and go from there?"

Mark grins widely at me. I bet he's already scheming about barbecues and Jeremy and next year's Pride getaway. And I know that whatever my plans for this year end up looking like, the final item on my bullet-pointed list will bring me right back here.

I can live with that.

ACKNOWLEDGMENTS

It's been almost ten years exactly since Robin Stevenson and I first crossed paths in beautiful Victoria, B.C. We were instant friends, and I missed her a great deal when I moved back to the east coast, so when she texted me out of the blue to propose writing a "big queer Canadian YA novel" together, it was a no-brainer. Writing this book was a pleasure in many ways, but above all else, it was an absolute treat to work on such a fun project with someone I admire and respect so much. I wouldn't say it was easy to write, but it came as close as any book has the right to!

I'm also grateful, as always, to my fabulous agent Eric Smith, for his hard work and advocacy. Thanks also to the whole gang at P.S. Literary for keeping the train on the tracks. A special thank you to Vee Signorelli for their insights and enthusiasm.

A huge thank you to Allison Cohen for seeing something special in our quirky little book, and the entire Running Press team, who have been wonderfully positive and enthusiastic about this project from day one.

Thank you to my parents, family, and friends who never fail to lift me up when I need it. A special shout out to my loved ones back home in Nova Scotia, and in particular in my hometown of Inverness. My support network is wide and deep and so very important to me. I love you all so much, and I'll never be able to give you proper thanks for your constant, energetic cheerleading.

Thank you to my friends in the writing and publishing world; there are too many names to mention, but you know who you are. This business can be tough, and it's honestly such a joy and a relief to belong to a community of people who "get it" and who are always ready to celebrate and commiserate as necessary. Thank you to the booksellers, librarians, reviewers, and bloggers who do so much to push and promote my books. I am so grateful for the often unseen work that you do—please know how much I appreciate it.

To the readers who keep coming back, book after book, especially the queer teens who write to tell me that they've found themselves in my stories, thank you. In all honesty, there is no higher compliment.

I'd be remiss if I didn't mention my sidekick and muse, Wheeler, who wakes me with a smile every morning, and knows just when to drag me out on a walk to figure out a complicated story issue. You are the very best boy. Finally, thank you to Andrew, who makes all of this possible. I love you, and I promise a sailboat is coming, even if I have to build it myself.

—TR

Huge thanks to my very good friend and brilliant writing partner, Tom Ryan. When we found ourselves living on opposite coasts, I missed him and wanted an excuse to talk more often . . . so one day I sent him a rather impulsive text to suggest writing a novel together. I am so glad I did and so glad he said yes! Writing together was great fun, and I'd do it again in a heartbeat.

I'd like to thank my agent, Eric Smith, for being such a pleasure to work with and for finding such a good publishing home for this book—and for the wonderful walking tour of Philadelphia during my too-brief visit. I am tremendously grateful for this opportunity to work with our editor, Allison Cohen, who brought so much enthusiasm and love for these characters along with her astute editorial advice. To everyone on the wonderful team at Running Press Kids, thank you for making this book look so beautiful and helping it find its readers. And to Chris King, the artist who created this stunning cover illustration— thank you so much. It is the perfect cover for the book.

Thanks also to the amazing Vee Signorelli for their enthusiasm and encouragement when I first told them about this project, and for their careful reading and insightful suggestions during the editing process nearly two years later. I have so much respect for their knowledge and expertise, and I am very grateful for their input. I am also grateful for all the work they have done to promote queer YA. It is thanks to advocates like Vee that books like this one are so much more possible now than they were just a decade ago.

To all the booksellers, librarians, teachers, bloggers, and reviewers who help get my books into the hands of readers, thank you! I so appreciate all you do. And to the readers themselves—thank you for making it possible for me to do what I love.

And finally, a huge and very grateful thank you to my friends and family for their endless support. My parents Ilse and Giles, my partner Cheryl, and my son Kai are there for me every day, and in so many ways. I couldn't be luckier. Love you all.

—RS